CLIFFSCOMPLETE™

Carroll's

Alice's Adventures in Wonderland

Edited and commentary by Bruce E. Walker

Professor of Literature, Popular Culture, and Academic Writing
University of Detroit Mercy, Detroit, Michigan

Complete Text + Commentary + Glossary

Hungry Minds™

HUNGRY MINDS, INC.

New York, NY • Cleveland, OH • Indianapolis, IN

Carroll's

Alice's Adventures in Wonderland

About the Author

Bruce Walker is a freelance writer who lives in Southeast Michigan, where he teaches literature, popular culture, and writing classes at the University of Detroit Mercy. Professor Walker also provides editorial and musical history consultation services to several clients in the Detroit area, and has written extensively on literature, automotive topics, film, music, and fly fishing. Professor Walker has also written a CliffsNotes on Ken Kesey's *One Flew Over the Cuckoo's Nest* published in December 2000.

Publisher's Acknowledgments

Editorial

Project Editor: Alissa D. Schwipps

Acquisitions Editor: Gregory W. Tubach

Copy Editor: Corey Dalton

Editorial Manager: Jennifer Ehrlich

Production

Indexer: Sharon Hilgenberg

Proofreader: Corey Bowen

Hungry Minds Indianapolis Production Services

Cover Illustration: Kate Dicker/Private Collection/Bridgeman Art Library. Used under license.

CliffsComplete™ *Alice's Adventures in Wonderland*

Published by:
Hungry Minds, Inc.
909 Third Avenue
New York, NY 10022

www.hungryminds.com (Hungry Minds, Inc. Web site)
www.cliffsnotes.com (CliffsNotes Web site)

Library of Congress Control Number: 2001024062

ISBN: 0-7645-8721-8

Printed in the United States of America

10 9 8 7 6 5 4 3 2 1

1O/RW/QU/QR/IN

Distributed in the United States by Hungry Minds, Inc.

Distributed by CDG Books Canada Inc. for Canada; by Transworld Publishers Limited in the United Kingdom; by IDG Norge Books for Norway; by IDG Sweden Books for Sweden; by IDG Books Australia Publishing Corporation Pty. Ltd. for Australia and New Zealand; by TransQuest Publishers Pte Ltd. for Singapore, Malaysia, Thailand, Indonesia, and Hong Kong; by Gotop Information Inc. for Taiwan; by ICG Muse, Inc. for Japan; by Norma Comunicaciones S.A. for Columbia; by Intersoft for South Africa; by Eyrolles for France; by International Thomson Publishing for Germany, Austria and Switzerland; by Distribuidora Cuspide for Argentina; by LR International for Brazil; by Galileo Libros for Chile; by Ediciones ZETA S.C.R. Ltda. for Peru; by WS Computer Publishing Corporation, Inc., for the Philippines; by Contemporanea de Ediciones for Venezuela; by Express Computer Distributors for the Caribbean and West Indies; by Micronesia Media Distributor, Inc. for Micronesia; by Grupo Editorial Norma S.A. for Guatemala; by Chips Computadoras S.A. de C.V. for Mexico; by Editorial Norma de Panama S.A. for Panama; by American Bookshops for Finland. Authorized Sales Agent: Anthony Rudkin Associates for the Middle East and North Africa.

For general information on Hungry Minds' products and services please contact our Customer Care department; within the U.S. at 800-762-2974, outside the U.S. at 317-572-3993 or fax 317-572-4002.

For sales inquiries and resellers information, including discounts, premium and bulk quantity sales, and foreign-language translations please contact our Customer Care department at 800-434-3422, fax 317-572-4002 or write to Hungry Minds, Inc., Attn: Customer Care department, 10475 Crosspoint Boulevard, Indianapolis, IN 46256.

For information on licensing foreign or domestic rights, please contact our Sub-Rights Customer Care department at 212-884-5000.

For information on using Hungry Minds' products and services in the classroom or for ordering examination copies, please contact our Educational Sales department at 800-434-2086 or fax 317-572-4005.

Please contact our Public Relations department at 212-884-5163 for press review copies or 212-884-5000 for author interviews and other publicity information or fax 212-884-5400.

For authorization to photocopy items for corporate, personal, or educational use, please contact Copyright Clearance Center, 222 Rosewood Drive, Danvers, MA 01923, or fax 978-750-4470.

Hungry Minds⁻ is a trademark of Hungry Minds, Inc.

CLIFFSCOMPLETE

Carroll's

Alice's Adventures in Wonderland

CONTENTS AT A GLANCE

CLIFFSCOMPLETE

Carroll's

Alice's Adventures in Wonderland

TABLE OF CONTENTS

ALICE'S ADVENTURES IN WONDERLAND

INTRODUCTION TO LEWIS CARROLL

Lewis Carroll was the pseudonym (or fictitious name) adopted by Charles Lutwidge Dodgson, the son of Charles Dodgson, a conservative pastor. Reverend Dodgson attended Christ Church, Oxford University, earning "Double Firsts" (or a double major) in Classics and Mathematics, lecturing and writing on both subjects. Because of his 1827 marriage to Frances Jane Lutwidge, however, Dodgson violated an Oxford requirement that all students remain celibate, and lost his appointment. Oxford then named Reverend Dodgson curate of All Saints Church in the rural and remote village of Daresbury Cheshire, England. The Dodgsons had eleven children during the next nineteen years, including their third child and first-born son, Charles.

Early life

Charles L. Dodgson was born January 27, 1832. His father is credited with nurturing the younger Dodgson's skills in mathematics, while his mother is believed to have inspired his religious and literary education. Dodgson's biographers believe the rural upbringing of his first eleven years remained the happiest of his life. In 1843, Reverend Dodgson accepted an appointment to the more accessible and affluent Croft and moved his family to North Yorkshire.

Home schooled for his first eleven years, Charles Dodgson exhibited his skills at mathematics, which he developed further at Richmond, a boarding school he attended when he was twelve years old. During this period, Dodgson

A portrait of English author Charles Lutwidge Dodgson (more popularly recognized by the pseudonym Lewis Carroll) circa 1863.
© Bettmann/CORBIS

wrote and sketched illustrated stories and plays for his siblings. When he was fourteen, Dodgson was enrolled at Rugby, where he confessed to be less happy than at Richmond. Some biographers speculate that he was a victim of sexual abuse at this time. Regardless, Dodgson mastered his studies and became increasingly adept at mathematics.

Professional life

In 1851, Charles Dodgson enrolled at Christ Church, Oxford, earning a Mastership in October 1855, and appointment as Christ Church Mathematical Lecturer. This last appointment Dodgson held for the next twenty-six years. In 1855, Dodgson also was introduced to the new photographic technologies, which sparked his interest in photography. Also in 1855, Dodgson met the new Dean of Christ Church, Henry Liddell. In 1856, Dodgson met Liddell's three daughters, including Alice, the inspiration for his most famous literary character.

Dodgson took Holy Orders and was ordained a deacon in December 1861, after attending Cuddleston Theological College. By this time, Dodgson had already completed his first three books on mathematics and had been publishing doggerel and poetry in several national magazines, including *The Train, The Comic Times*, the *Whitby Gazette,* and the *Oxford Critic.* Edmund Yates, the editor of *The Train,* asked Dodgson to create a pseudonym, and he complied with four possible candidates, one of which was Lewis Carroll.

Dodgson's interest in photography increased in 1856 when he bought his first camera. His subjects included England's Poet Laureate Alfred Lord Tennyson, Dante Gabriel Rossetti,

Christina Rossetti, and the Liddell sisters. His trademark photographic subject, however, was young girls in various stages of undress, which has inspired much speculation that Dodgson was a pedophile—despite the fact that all of these photographic sessions had parental consent and, furthermore, none of his subjects ever reported inappropriate advances from Dodgson. Regardless, no conclusive evidence exists to support any charges of impropriety against Dodgson.

On July 4, 1862, Dodgson, his friend Robinson Duckworth, and sisters Ina, Alice, and Edith Liddell took one of several boat trips on the Isis River. This particular trip differed from the others because Dodgson related the outline

Portrait of the original Alice in Wonderland, Alice Liddell.
© Bettmann/CORBIS

of the story that would become *Alice's Adventures in Wonderland* to his companions. On subsequent trips, Dodgson embellished the story, and some months later composed an eighteen-thousand-word manuscript originally entitled *Alice's Adventures Under Ground* with his own illustrations. He later commissioned *Punch* magazine illustrator John Tenniel to create original artwork. In 1865, Macmillan published *Alice's Adventures in Wonderland* to nearly unanimous praise.

By 1866, *Alice's Adventures in Wonderland* was already in its third printing and, the following year, French and German translations were published. An Italian translation was published in 1868. Dodgson published the further adventures of Alice, *Through the Looking-Glass: And What Alice Found There*, in 1872. He followed this work with the mock epic, *The Hunting of the Snark: An Agony in Eight Fits*, in 1876. His final work of fiction, the two-part novel, *Sylvie and Bruno* and *Sylvie and Bruno: Concluded*, was published, respectively, in 1889 and 1893.

Personal life

The success of Dodgson's work would have catapulted him to celebrity status had he not scrupulously remained incognito behind the pseudonym Lewis Carroll. Letters he received addressed to Lewis Carroll were returned unopened. Nevertheless, the success of *Alice's Adventures in Wonderland* prompted him to write its sequel, despite having lost his friendship with his original muse, Alice Liddell.

Dodgson's relationship with the Liddell family has been a source of speculation among his biographers. Many of these authors discuss the rumors surrounding Dodgson's intentions toward the young Alice; some suggest that his feelings toward her were merely platonic, but others allege that Alice's parents rebuked Dodgson when he requested her hand in marriage. Regardless, a rift in the relationship between Dodgson and the Liddells is evident as early as 1863 and, by 1864, Mrs. Liddell refused Dodgson's requests to take the sisters on further boating excursions. Although Dodgson communicated with the younger Liddell afterwards and well into her adulthood, the intimacy between the two was never revived.

Dodgson's personal friendships during this period of his life consisted mainly of visual artists and other writers. He befriended, or at the very least became personally acquainted with, many of the most notable Pre-Raphaelites painters and writers, including Dante Gabriel Rossetti, William Morris, Charles Algernon Swinburne, and Edward Burne-Jones. In 1863, Dodgson visited Rossetti and photographed the painter and his sister, the poet Christina Rossetti. John Ruskin and George MacDonald number among his other literary and artistic friends, acquaintances or photographic subjects. He included among his favorite photographic subjects the sisters Kate and Ellen Terry, both renowned for their physical beauty.

Dodgson continued to lecture on mathematics at Christ Church until he gave it up in 1881. During this time, he also abandoned his passion for photography, presumably to dedicate more time to his writing. He was an ardent theatergoer until his later years when he refused to view productions that he believed promoted immoral behavior. Throughout his adult life, he was known as a fastidious man with a chronic stammer and a gift for befriending young women, including Ellen Terry, Isa Bowman, and Enid Stevens, until his death from pneumonia in 1898 at age sixty-six.

Selected writings

As Charles Lutwidge Dodgson:

A Syllabus of Plane Algebraical Geometry, Part I (1860)

The Formulae of Plane Trigonometry (1861)

An Elementary Treatise on Determinants (1867)

The Fifth Book of Euclid Treated Algebraically (1868)

Euclid and His Modern Rivals (1879)

Supplement to "Euclid and His Modern Rivals" (1879)

Uncredited or Anonymous:

The New Method of Evaluation as Applied to Pi (1865)

The Dynamics of a Particle (1865)

As Lewis Carroll:

Alice's Adventures in Wonderland (1865)

Phantasmagoria and Other Poems (1869)

Through the Looking-Glass: And What Alice Found There (1872)

The Hunting of the Snark: An Agony in Eight Fits (1876)

Doublets: A Word-Puzzle (1879)

Rhyme? And Reason? (1883)

A Tangled Tale (1885)

The Nursery Alice (1889)

Sylvie and Bruno (1889)

Sylvie and Bruno: Concluded (1893)

INTRODUCTION TO *ALICE'S ADVENTURES IN WONDERLAND*

Alice's Adventures in Wonderland, commonly known as *Alice in Wonderland* after the several film adaptations inspired by the original work, is alternately revered as a work of childhood whimsy and nonsense and as a satirical examination of the nature of language, Victorian morality, and the vagaries of the English legal system. The work and its sequel—*Through the Looking-Glass: And What Alice Found There*—are among the first works of children's fiction to entertain both youths and adults on their respective levels.

Historical context of the novel

Alice's Adventures in Wonderland was inspired by events that occurred in 1862, considered a midway point of the English Victorian era. Children during the Victorian era did not receive special privileges, and were often treated as smaller versions of adults. For example, many children were discouraged from reading fantasies and fairy tales during this period because many Victorians believed that literature should relate realistic stories that advocated valuable life lessons. These lessons instructed children on how to behave like responsible adults. Many Victorian students were forced to memorize the moral lessons of Robert Southey's "The Old Man's Comforts, and How He Gained Them," Isaac Watt's "The Sluggard" and "Against Idleness and Mischief," and Mary Howitt's "The Spider and the Fly." Carroll hilariously parodies the didacticism (preachiness) of these poems when he has Alice recite them incorrectly.

The Victorian value placed upon children either to "be seen and not heard" or to behave like adults is illustrated by photographs of children taken during this era. Many of these photographs, including some taken by Carroll himself, depict children dressed in adult attire rather than in children's play clothes. Some critics attribute the decreased value Victorians placed upon children and the desire to consider them adults as responses to the high mortality rates of children under the age of seven.

If the combined effect of the memorized morality stories and the adoption of adult fashion in photography reveals the Victorian era's attempt to force adult behavior on children, the depiction of adult behavior toward children who insist on being seen and heard in *Alice's Adventures in Wonderland* is equally revealing. Adults eagerly adopt authority over Alice who admits to being a little girl. Beginning with the Lory, who says that he knows better than Alice by benefit of his being older than she, and including the Duchess' incessant moralizing and the abuse of authority displayed by the King and Queen of Hearts, *Alice's Adventures in Wonderland* contains many displays of autocratic and arbitrary power by adults.

As noted by critic William Empson in his article titled "Alice in Wonderland," another historical factor reflected in *Alice's Adventures in Wonderland* is the discovery of the first Neanderthal (a prehistoric primate believed by some to have eventually evolved into the human species) skull and the evolutionary theories of Charles Darwin. Darwin published his famous work, *Origin of the Species,* in 1859, three years before Carroll conceived *Alice's Adventures in Wonderland* and six years before he published *Alice*. Empson equates Alice's plunge into her Pool of Tears with humankind arising from a primordial soup. In fact, when Alice leaves the pool, Empson says "Noah's Ark gets out of the sea with her." (Chatto and Windus, 1935) Empson also suggests that Carroll's inclusion of the Dodo (a large, flightless bird extinct long before the publication of *Alice*) refers to Darwin's theories of the stronger species surviving longer than weaker species.

Alice as a children's book

As a children's book, *Alice's Adventures in Wonderland* presents a precocious little seven-year-old girl who abandons her sister, her cat, and the world of rational behavior (although never the world of rational expectations) when she chases a vest-wearing rabbit down a hole. Her adventures lead her to encounters with several talking animals, anthropomorphic (or humanlike) playing cards, argumentative and often violent characters, and people of questionable sanity. Although these characters often exude an almost sinister quality, Carroll redeems most of them by depicting them in a humorous and even ridiculous fashion, rendering them merely ludicrous.

Public recognition of *Alice's Adventures in Wonderland* in the twentieth century and beyond is due largely to the softening of Carroll's semantic and legal themes at the expense of a kinder and more inoffensive depiction of many of its characters in several cinematic adaptations. At the hands of animators and casting directors, these characters lose much of their more bizarre and outlandish characteristics in favor of renderings that are more suitable for plush toys. Indeed, even some of Alice's more objectionable qualities are mediated to make her more agreeable to post-Victorian audiences. For example, Carroll's Alice exhibits signs of upper middle-class snobbishness when the Mock Turtle and Gryphon discuss the "extras" of their schooling. For the Turtle and Gryphon, extras (presumably extracurricular studies) means washing. When the pair asks Alice if her extras included washing (by which they mean laundry, a menial task), Alice becomes, in Carroll's words, "indignant." Alice's indignation reveals that she considers washing beneath her social status. In film versions, however, Alice is seldom depicted as a class-conscious snob, but rather a voice of reason in a world governed by madness.

Although the story contains many violent elements that support philosopher Bertrand Russell's contention that the book should never be read by anyone under the age of nineteen, other elements of the novel soften the story's violent content. In fact, *Alice's Adventures in*

Wonderland is book-ended by Carroll's opening poem that idealizes youth and the day he began telling the Wonderland story to the Liddell sisters and the closing paragraphs of Alice's sister contemplating the fleeting youth of Alice and whether Alice will maintain her imagination into adulthood.

Alice as a work of imaginative fantasy and nonsense

The study of the *Alice* books as examples of imaginative and nonsense literature in the manner of poet Edward Lear has been one of several critical approaches to the works since their publication. That both *Alice* books are revealed to be dreams and display the often-distorted logic of the dream state frequently is the approach taken by critics.

In the world of Wonderland, it is taken for granted that characters can change their physical size, and that their clothing will change proportionally as well. In Wonderland, it is not challenged that animals and such inanimate objects as playing cards are anthropomorphized until the final chapter of *Alice's Adventures in Wonderland*. Such fantastic elements are balanced against the nonsensical qualities of flamingoes and hedgehogs used as the instruments of a croquet game, disappearing cats, and sisters living at the bottom of a treacle well.

Carroll also enjoys using puns and double entendres (or terms with two meanings, especially when one meaning is risqué) to heighten the nonsense of Alice (as is discussed later in this introduction). For example, Wonderland is a place where a defendant is sentenced before a verdict is rendered, and a poem making no sense whatsoever is treated as irrefutable evidence of the Knave of Hearts' guilt in stealing the Queen's tarts.

In addressing the nonsensical qualities of *Alice's Adventures in Wonderland*, G. K. Chesterton wrote in his essay titled "Lewis Carroll": "[Carroll] took his triangles and turned them into toys for a favourite little girl; he took his logarithms and syllogisms and twisted them into nonsense." (Sheed and Ward, 1953) Chesterton believed, however, that the nonsense exhibited in *Alice* served no other purpose than to entertain the reader with Carroll's cleverness. For instance, Chesterton claims that the nonsensical qualities of works by Rabelais and Jonathon Swift are employed to satirical effect. Not so with Carroll, according to Chesterton. Chesterton asserts that Carroll's "genius" lay in his ability to use nonsense as a means to invert commonly held logical assumptions. Chesterton's analysis reveals his belief that Carroll intended his work solely for the purpose of entertainment and not enlightenment nor education.

Edmund Wilson, in his essay "C. L. Dodgson: The Poet Logician," disagrees with critics who assert, "the *Alice* that grownups read is really a different work from the *Alice* that is read by children." (Farrar, Straus & Giroux, Inc., 1952) Wilson believed that children and adults alike could discern that both works display the imagination's ability to distort reality while at the same time reinforcing it. In other words, Wilson says that by contrasting the real world with the events, actions, and settings of Wonderland, the reader becomes more aware of reality.

Wilson continued, "The shiftings and the transformations, the mishaps and the triumphs of Alice's dream, the mysteries and the riddles, the gibberish that conveys unmistakable meanings, are all based upon relationships that contradict the assumptions of our conscious lives but that are lurking not far behind them." Thus,

Wilson believes that reality is reinforced when the reader compares it to the topsy-turvy world of Wonderland.

Perhaps Walter de la Mare captures the nonsensical essence of the *Alice* books most succinctly when he wrote in *Lewis Carroll:* "Carroll's Wonderland indeed is a (queer little) universe of the mind resembling Einstein's in that it is a finite infinity endlessly explorable though never to be explored." (Faber and Faber Ltd., 1932) The critic captures a paradoxical element that is prevalent throughout the works. The laws of nature are turned against themselves time and time again by Alice's size-altering, which is induced by her ingestion of mushrooms, potions, and stones that turn into cakes. Royalty rules for no apparent reason other than the nominalist rule that they are called kings and queens and must, therefore, serve as rulers. Logic itself is determined by those individuals best able to thwart the laws of logical discourse.

Alice, wordplay, and the nature of language

Perhaps as common as the perception of *Alice's Adventures in Wonderland* as a work for children or source material for cinematic purposes is the interpretation of the book as a study in the nature of language. In fact, *Alice's Adventures in Wonderland* has been source material for literary and philosophical works since its publication. According to many of these works, *Alice's Adventures in Wonderland* points out the inability of language to accurately convey precisely what the human transmitter intends.

Among the writers who borrowed freely from Carroll's work to explore the nature of language are the Austrian-English philosopher Ludwig Wittgenstein, English philosopher

Bertrand Russell, novelist Paul Auster (whose *City of Glass* actually names one of its characters H. D. after Humpty Dumpty in *Through the Looking-Glass: And What Alice Found There*), and science-fiction short-story writer Henry Kuttner (Kuttner's short story, "Mimsey Were the Borogroves," postulates that the language of Carroll's poem "Jabberwocky" is actually a language understood only by children whose minds have not been structured according to Euclidean logic).

For many readers, Alice is a representation of humans who cannot express accurately the difference between logic and illogic as well as the inherent traps and shortcomings of language. In Wonderland, Alice struggles to differentiate between saying what she means and her assertion that she means what she says. She fails in either case, as the Mad Hatter and White Rabbit point out in Chapter VII.

Language is a hodgepodge of signs reliant upon the refinement of the transmitter as well as the listening and interpretive abilities of the human receiver. A "disconnect" will lead to misinterpretation and misunderstanding. Such a disconnect can be caused by the imprecise nature of the language employed, or can be intensified by confused signals between the speaker and the listener such as tone of voice, physical expressions, or context.

Language is furthermore subject to idiomatic expressions, vernacular usage, and varieties of pronunciation, all of which can cause the intention of the speaker to be lost or misconstrued by the listener. As language develops, other elements contribute to the spoken and written words' inability to convey precisely the intent of the speaker. These elements include such literary devices as puns and double entendres (words with double meanings), homonyms (a word with the same pronunciation as another but with a different meaning), malapropisms (the ludicrous misuse of words especially through confusion caused by resemblance in sound), and antonyms (words with opposite meanings). The nature of communication is, therefore, not a simple accomplishment, which Carroll playfully exploits throughout *Alice's Adventures in Wonderland*.

When Alice plummets down the hole in Chapter I, she considers her whereabouts with the first of the story's many malapropisms. Believing herself to be falling through and past the Earth's center, she wonders if she is in the Antipodes, which as a common noun denotes two opposite ends of the globe, or, as a proper noun, New Zealand and Australia. What she says, however, is "antipathies," which, although resembling the sound of "antipodes," is clearly something else altogether. The humor of the malapropism lies in the denotation of the word "antipathy" in place of "antipodes," as antipathy means an aversion to something. In Alice's case, this aversion could be to her falling in the first place.

Carroll again depicts Alice using language that she clearly does not understand when she considers her Latitude and Longitude. In one of several authorial intrusions in the story, he tells the reader: "Alice had not the slightest idea what Latitude was, or Longitude either, but she thought they were nice grand words to say." Later, she ponders words separated from the object and function that they are intended to signify when she inverts the phrase, "Do cats eat bats?" to "Do bats eat cats?" Untethered from their ascribed subjects, the words and the phrase become meaningless. In either case, Alice doesn't know the answer to the question, and because no one is present to answer the question in the first place, the phrasing of the question makes no difference.

In Chapter II, Alice, freed from the restrictions of proper grammar, defies the rules of diction by declaring her situation to be "curiouser and curiouser." She then proceeds to violate the rules of polite language by inquiring of the Mouse in the only French phrase she remembers, "Ou est ma chatte?" or "Where is my cat?" By offending the Mouse, Alice learns that words have the power to frighten or incite others. She accidentally compounds her offense when she begins telling a harmless story of her neighbor's dog, which concludes with her boast that the pet is responsible for the death of many rodents. This misjudgment further worries the Mouse, who equates the signifiers "cat" and "dog" with the actual animate forms commonly known as a cat and a dog and the actions commonly associated with such animals; namely, the killing and eating of rodents. The Mouse tells Alice, "As if *I* would talk on such a subject! Our family always *hated* cats: nasty, low, vulgar things! Don't let me hear the name again!" Again, the Mouse mistakenly equates Alice's mentioning the word "cat" with an actual, living creature. Because an actual cat would eat a mouse, the Mouse is frightened, even though Alice has only used the word "cat" and no cat is actually present.

In Chapter III, Carroll begins his wordplay with a pun on the word dry. Dry, the opposite of wet, is also used as an adjective to describe a subject that is dull and boring. When the Mouse offers to help his soaked comrades dry, he proceeds to tell them "the driest thing I know." The Mouse tells his story—an entirely uninteresting piece of English history—and is challenged by the Duck over the use of the pronoun "it." Because the Mouse's recital does not include a previous reference for the use of "it," in the phrase "found it advisable," the Duck demands to know what "it" signifies. In this instance, "found" does not represent that the characters in the Mouse's story actually "found" or "discovered" something (it), but that they "determined" or "decided" that "it" was advisable. But the Duck objects that when the Duck finds something ("it"), "it's generally a frog, or a worm." This confusion over the different uses of "common" language reveals that language is only common insofar as all involved in the communication agree upon certain linguistic suppositions.

Echoing Alice's use of the words "Longitude" and "Latitude" that she doesn't understand in Chapter I, the Dodo speaks in language that is inflated and abstract, "I move that the meeting adjourn, for the immediate adoption of more energetic remedies." He suggests a Caucus-race, although he cannot describe what it is. "The best way to explain it is to do it," he tells Alice. In this, he substitutes an action for a definition because language would be a longer and, inevitably, poorer substitute for depicting what a Caucus-race is.

The remainder of Chapter III involves the misunderstanding of the homonyms "tale" and "tail" and "not" and "knot." Alice repeats her previous mistake of mentioning her cat, Dinah, resulting in the remaining animals abandoning her in haste.

In Chapter V, Alice argues with the Caterpillar over the nature of identity, which is presumably a philosophical argument. However, the language employed by both the Caterpillar and Alice leads to confusion as to what information the pair wishes to exchange. When the Caterpillar asks, "Who are you?" he isn't asking Alice for a statement of being, he only wishes to know her name and, perhaps, function. The many physical changes enacted upon Alice, however, lead her to answer that she is unaware of her identity. She emphasizes to the Caterpillar that these changes have been rapid, unexpected, and uncomfortable. Because the Caterpillar anticipates such changes as part of a caterpillar's nature, he cannot agree with her. Alice grows impatient with what she perceives to be the contradictory nature of the Caterpillar, but she fails to realize that their failure to communicate results from their differing physical natures, not in the language they employ.

When Alice encounters the Pigeon, the two engage in a conversation concerning appearances and the relation of appearance to the actual nature of an animate being and, thus, what that being is named or called. Alice declares that she is a little girl. Stating that her declaration is contrary to her appearance, the Pigeon asserts that Alice, whose neck is recently elongated from her ingestion of the mushroom, is a serpent. The Pigeon employs a syllogism (two distinct phrases used to prove a third statement) to prove that Alice is a serpent. It reasons that, if Alice looks like a serpent and eats eggs; she must be, in fact, a serpent.

In Chapter VI, Alice mistakenly believes that external factors can alter the identity of a creature. She refuses to call a fish and a frog by their proper names or classifications because they are dressed as footmen. Of course, both footmen are really animals, but Alice believes that their human clothing makes them human with animal characteristics. Similarly, she makes the same mistake when she takes the baby from the Duchess, and later discovers it is a pig. An ugly baby, perhaps, Alice thinks, but a grand pig. In both instances, Alice presumes that the creatures (the Fish, the Frog, and the Pig) can be called human because they wear human clothing and (in the case of the footmen) use human language. However, Alice's assumption is incorrect.

The precise use of language requires that each animal still be classified by its correct species, whereas a more abstract language could classify them as human.

The abstract nature of language also is displayed by Alice's first conversation with the Cheshire Cat. Alice asks the Cat for directions, but doesn't specify where she wants to go. Stating, "that depends a good deal on where you want to get to," the Cat is told that Alice only wants to "get *somewhere.*" The Cat, very rightly, tells Alice that she's certain to arrive somewhere by walking in any direction long enough. Alice tries another approach with the literal-minded Cat by asking him who lives nearby. The Cat responds that the Mad Hatter's house is close, but warns Alice that he is insane. He says that the March Hare also lives nearby, but that he, too, is insane.

When Alice arrives at the March Hare's house in Chapter VII, the Hare is having tea with the Mad Hatter and the Dormouse. The veracity of language is called into question immediately as the trio lies to the young girl that there is no room for her at the table when obviously there is room. She is then offered wine, an offer that the trio has no intention of granting because they have no wine to offer. In both instances, it is revealed to Alice that the trio uses language dishonestly, which should put her on her toes for her subsequent conversation with them.

When Alice tells the tea party that she can guess the answer to the Hatter's riddle, the Hare challenges her phrasing, "Do you mean that you think you can find out the answer to it?" and tells her that she "should say what [she] means." Alice responds that she does say what she means, "at least—at least I mean what I say—that's the same thing, you know." The group points out the error in her logic—the two statements do not mean the same thing.

More misunderstandings occur when Alice refers to "killing time" in the vernacular sense, but the Hatter misconstrues her meaning as he has a personal relationship with an anthropomorphized Time. The group asks the Dormouse to tell a story that is rife with puns. In his story, three sisters live at the bottom of a treacle-well. Treacle is a sweet molasses that is processed from sorghum rather than taken from a well, which is a hole in the ground from which such liquids as water or oil are extracted. Because the Dormouse has committed his story's absurd setting to a treacle well, he responds that the sisters draw treacle from the well in which they live. If one draws water from a regular well, it is reasonable to assume that the sisters would draw treacle from a treacle well. The Dormouse puns on the word "draw" here by saying that the sisters are learning to draw, denoting the construction of a visual representation or picture. When Alice points out that the sisters live in the well, a statement that seemingly refutes the Dormouse's assertion that the sisters live in a well from which they can draw treacle, the Dormouse responds affirmatively with another pun; that the sisters were "well in," an idiomatic expression for fatigue.

Perhaps the most outrageous example of punning, malapropisms, and use of homonyms exists in Chapter IX, in which the Mock Turtle and Gryphon abuse the language in a manner seldom equaled in literature. The Mock Turtle tells of his old school master, an old turtle the students called "Tortoise," because he "taught us." The classes taught at the school consist of Reeling and Writhing, malapropisms for Reading and Writing. He mentions that the Gryphon's master, described as an old crab, taught Laughing and Grief, malapropisms for Latin and Greek.

The numerous examples of wordplay in *Alice's Adventures in Wonderland* display how human language can be misunderstood and misinterpreted to comic effect. Many of Carroll's puns and malapropisms are hilarious, particularly when placed in the mouths of the Gryphon and Mock Turtle. Regardless, the speaker Carroll chooses to mouth his intentional communicative mistakes, however, each instance serves to point out that verbal communication is an imprecise and often misunderstood medium.

Psychological interpretations of *Alice*

The advent of psychology in the twentieth century has led to many readings of *Alice* intended to either place the work as an enlightened analysis of a young person's stages of development or as revelatory of Carroll's phobias and fetishes. As early as the 1920s and 1930s, such critics as psychologist Andre Tridon, psychoanalyst Paul Schilder, and literary critic Joseph Wood Krutch debated the merits of psychological interpretations of Carroll's fiction.

Among some hypotheses concerning Carroll is that his background as a reverend's son was repressive and that he was frequently subjected to psychological or even physical brutality. Among the evidence used to defend this hypothesis is the characters of the King and Queen of Hearts. Their autocratic abuse of power most closely resembles the authority parents might exert over their children. Schilder believes that Carroll may not have received "the full love of his parents."

Schilder finds many examples of "oral aggressiveness" and "oral sadism" in the story, namely the propensity of many of the characters to eat each other or the threat of being eaten by another animal. By "oral aggressiveness," these psychoanalysts mean that the characters threaten violence using their mouths and teeth. For example, Alice scares the Mouse and the Dodo, Eaglet, and other birds by discussing how her cat and her neighbor's dog are good at catching and eating birds and rodents. Schilder also argues that Alice always is wanting for food, because whatever she does ingest only serves to alter her size and shape instead of satiating her hunger or thirst. Schilder writes, "We are accustomed to find such dreams in persons with strong repressions which prevent final satisfactions," believing that Carroll is revealing his unrealized worldly desires; namely, the love of his parents. Because Carroll was the eldest boy in a large family that lived in poverty for the better part of his upbringing, Schilder believes Carroll was denied the attentions of his parents.

The continuous changing of Alice's physique also is interpreted as an indication of extreme anxiety concerning body image. Alice is either too big or too small for many of the encounters she experiences. Schilder perceives this fact as phallic symbolism, and also believes that Carroll may have substituted young girls for his incestuous affections for his mother and sisters. He concludes that Carroll's employment of nonsense represents his regressive tendencies and, like Sigmund Freud, Schilder believes that nonsense betrays a hostile and aggressive nature. He finds that the *Alice* stories contain very little of a constructive and loving nature.

Violence in *Alice*

American novelist Katherine Anne Porter considered *Alice* "a horror story. . . it frightened me so much, and I didn't know then whether it was the pictures or the text. Rereading it, I should think it was the text. . . . It was a terrible mixture of suffering and cruelty and rudeness and false logic and traps for the innocent—in fact, awful." (Random House, 1942)

The story begins with Alice plummeting down a hole, a frightening enough adventure for an adult, much less a child. She then inadvertently offends the Mouse, the Dodo, the Eagle, the Duck and others by discussing her cat, Dinah, and her neighbor's dog, about whose abilities to catch and eat birds and rodents she boasts. Alice boots Bill the Lizard sky high from the chimney before encountering a gargantuan puppy, which she fears will crush her with its playfulness. She travels to the Duchess' house, where a baby is abused and a cook violently throws things at Alice, the baby, and the Duchess. Elsewhere, the Mad Hatter is said to be murdering a personified Time. The Queen of Hearts wishes everyone beheaded during the croquet game and the King of Hearts ponders how to behead the Cheshire Cat, who shows only his head to begin with.

English philosopher Bertrand Russell believed that *Alice* is best read by children over the age of fifteen. And his point and Porter's observation are well taken, as *Alice* contains many violent scenes as well as threats of violence against Alice and the other characters. Some of this broadly depicted violence, however, is meant to convey humor, much like the cartoon violence of the Three Stooges, Monty Python's Flying Circus, and the Warner Brothers' animated comedies.

Critical and public reception of *Alice*

Since its publication in 1865, *Alice's Adventures in Wonderland* has had its share of critical champions and detractors. An anonymous critic wrote in *The Athenaeum* magazine in 1865 that *Alice* was a "stiff, over-wrought story." Despite this negative review, *Alice's Adventures in Wonderland* enjoyed tremendous popular success that inspired the sequel, *Through the Looking-Glass: And What Alice Found There.* When the Dodgson's estate copyright expired on *Alice* during the first decade of the twentieth century, dozens of publishers commissioned their own artwork to accompany their editions of the story, which brought the story before an even larger public audience. The story continues to delight children and adults in the twenty-first century.

Not until the twentieth century, however, was serious critical attention given to Carroll's *Alice* books. Among the first critics to recognize Carroll's fictional works as serious works of literature is William Empson. Empson is perhaps the first critic to apply the psychological theories of Sigmund Freud to *Alice*, an approach since followed by many others, including Paul Schilder. Many of these critics attempt to uncover elements of Carroll's psyche. Other critical approaches to *Alice* include the insecurities of children growing into puberty, the nature of identity, the examination of space and time, and the search for organizing principles in a disorganized world.

CHARACTERS IN THE BOOK

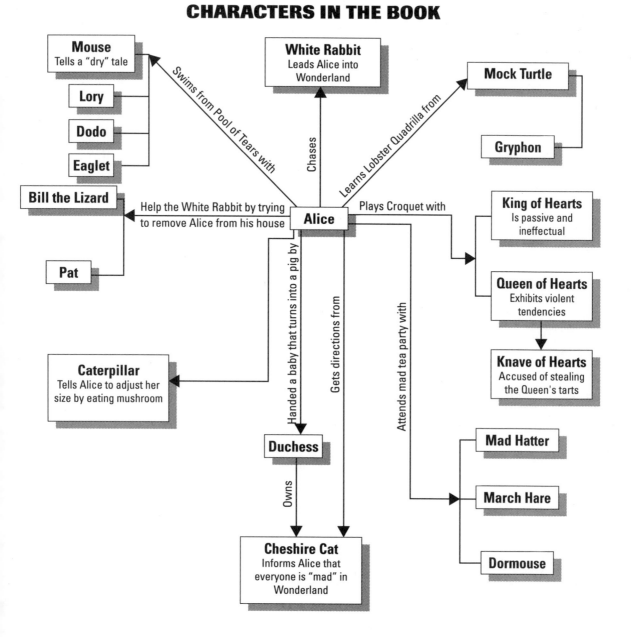

CLIFFSCOMPLETE

ALICE'S ADVENTURES IN WONDERLAND

Chapter I: Down the Rabbit-Hole

Feeling sleepy while sitting on a riverbank with her sister, Alice follows a waist-coat wearing White Rabbit down a rabbit-hole, ends up in a hall of doors she can't open, and shrinks to ten inches in height.

All in the golden afternoon
　　Full leisurely we glide;
For both our oars, with little skill,
　　By little arms are plied,
While little hands make vain pretence
　　Our wanderings to guide.

Ah, cruel Three! In such an hour
　　Beneath such dreamy weather,
To beg a take of breath too weak
　　To stir the tiniest feather!
Yet what can one poor voice agail
　　Against three tongues together?

Imperious Prima flashes forth
　　Her edict 'to begin it' —
In gentler tone Secunda hopes
　　'There will be nonsense in it!' —
While Tertia interrupts the tale
　　Not more than once a minute.

Anon, to sudden silence won,
　　In fancy they pursue
The dream-child moving through a land
　　Of wonders whild and new,
In friendly chat with bird or beast —
　　And half belive it true.

And ever, as the story drained
　　The wells of fancy dry,
And faintly stove that weary one
　　To put the suhject by,

'The rest next time —' 'It is next time!'
   The happy voices cry.

Thus grew the tale of Wonderland:
   Thus slowly, one by one,
Its quaint events were hammered out —
   And now the tale is done,
And home we steer, a merry crew,
   Beneath the setting sun.

Alice! A childish story take,
   And with a gentle hand
Lay it where Childhood's dreams are twined
   In Memory's mystic band,
Like pilgrim's wither'd wreath of flowers
   Pluck'd in a far-off land.

Alice was beginning to get very tired of sitting by
   her sister on the bank, and of having nothing to
   do: once or twice she had peeped into the book
   her sister was reading, but it had no pictures or
   conversations in it, "and what is the use of a
   book," thought Alice, "without pictures or
   conversation?"
So she was considering in her own mind (as well
   as she could, for the hot day made her feel very
   sleepy and stupid), whether the pleasure of making a daisy-chain would be worth the trouble of
   getting up and picking the daisies, when suddenly a White Rabbit with pink eyes ran close
   by her.
There was nothing so very remarkable in that;
   nor did Alice think it so very much out of the
   way to hear the Rabbit say to itself, "Oh dear!
   Oh dear! I shall be late!" (when she thought it
   over afterwards, it occurred to her that she ought
   to have wondered at this, but at the time it all
   seemed quite natural); but when the Rabbit

*A frantic White Rabbit hurries to keep his appointment with
the Queen.*
Mary Evans Picture Library

actually took a watch out of its **waistcoat**-pocket, and looked at it, and then hurried on, Alice started to her feet, for it flashed across her mind that she had never before seen a rabbit with either a waistcoat-pocket, or a watch to take out of it, and burning with curiosity, she ran across the field after it, and fortunately was just in time to see it pop down a large rabbit-hole under the **hedge.**

In another moment down went Alice after it, never once considering how in the world she was to get out again.

The rabbit-hole went straight on like a tunnel for some way, and then dipped suddenly down, so suddenly that Alice had not a moment to think about stopping herself before she found herself falling down a very deep well.

Either the well was very deep, or she fell very slowly, for she had plenty of time as she went down to look about her and to wonder what was going to happen next. First, she tried to look down and make out what she was coming to, but it was too dark to see anything; then she looked at the sides of the well, and noticed that they were filled with cupboards and book-shelves; here and there she saw maps and pictures hung upon pegs. She took down a jar from one of the shelves as she passed; it was labeled "ORANGE **MARMALADE**," but to her great disappointment it was empty: she did not like to drop the jar for fear of killing somebody, so managed to put it into one of the cupboards as she fell past it.

"Well!" thought Alice to herself, "after such a fall as this, I shall think nothing of tumbling down stairs! How brave they'll all think me at home! Why, I wouldn't say anything about it, even if I fell off the top of the house!" (Which was very likely true.)

waistcoat: a somewhat longer, heavily ornamented sleeveless jacket formerly worn under a doublet.

hedge: a row of closely planted shrubs, bushes, or trees forming a boundary or fence.

marmalade: a jam-like preserve made by boiling the pulp and usually the sliced-up rinds of oranges or some other fruit with sugar.

Down, down, down. Would the fall never come to an end! "I wonder how many miles I've fallen by this time?" she said aloud. "I must be getting somewhere near the centre of the earth. Let me see: that would be four thousand miles down, I think — " (for, you see, Alice had learnt several things of this sort in her lessons in the schoolroom, and though this was not a very good opportunity for showing off her knowledge, as there was no one to listen to her, still it was good practice to say it over) " — yes, that's about the right distance — but then I wonder what **Latitude** or **Longitude** I've got to?" (Alice had no idea what Latitude was, or Longitude either, but thought they were nice grand words to say.) Presently she began again. "I wonder if I shall fall right through the earth! How funny it'll seem to come out among the people that walk with their heads downward! The **Antipathies,** I think — " (she was rather glad there was no one listening, this time, as it didn't sound at all the right word) " — but I shall have to ask them what the name of the country is, you know. Please, Ma'am, is this New Zealand or Australia?" (and she tried to curtsey as she spoke — fancy curtseying as you're falling through the air! Do you think you could manage it?) "And what an ignorant little girl she'll think me for asking! No, it'll never do to ask: perhaps I shall see it written up somewhere." Down, down, down. There was nothing else to do, so Alice soon began talking again. "Dinah'll miss me very much to-night, I should think!" (Dinah was the cat.) "I hope they'll remember her saucer of milk at tea-time. Dinah my dear! I wish you were down here with me! There are no mice in the air, I'm afraid, but you might catch a bat, and that's very like a mouse, you know. But do cats eat bats, I wonder?" And here Alice

latitude: the angular distance, measured in degrees, north or south from the equator.

longitude: the distance east or west on the earth's surface, measured as an arc of the equator (in degrees up to 180 degrees or by the difference in time) between the meridian passing through a particular place and a standard or prime meridian, usually the one passing through Greenwich, England.

Antipathies: a malapropism, or mispronunciation, of Antipodes, which is a place on the opposite side of the earth—in this instance, New Zealand and Australia.

began to get rather sleepy, and went on saying to herself, in a dreamy sort of way, "Do cats eat bats? Do cats eat bats?" and sometimes, "Do bats eat cats?" for, you see, as she couldn't answer either question, it didn't much matter which way she put it. She felt that she was dozing off, and had just begun to dream that she was walking hand in hand with Dinah, and saying to her very earnestly, "Now, Dinah, tell me the truth: did you ever eat a bat?" when suddenly, thump! thump! down she came upon a heap of sticks and dry leaves, and the fall was over.

Alice was not a bit hurt, and she jumped up on to her feet in a moment: she looked up, but it was all dark overhead; before her was another long passage, and the White Rabbit was still in sight, hurrying down it. There was not a moment to be lost: away went Alice like the wind, and was just in time to hear it say, as it turned a corner, "Oh my ears and whiskers, how late it's getting!" She was close behind it when she turned the corner, but the Rabbit was no longer to be seen: she found herself in a long, low hall, which was lit up by a row of lamps hanging from the roof.

There were doors all round the hall, but they were all locked; and when Alice had been all the way down one side and up the other, trying every door, she walked sadly down the middle, wondering how she was ever to get out again. Suddenly she came upon a little three-legged table, all made of solid glass; there was nothing on it except a tiny golden key, and Alice's first thought was that it might belong to one of the doors of the hall; but, alas! either the locks were too large, or the key was too small, but at any rate it would not open any of them. However, on the second time round, she came upon a low curtain she had not noticed before, and behind it was a little door about fifteen inches high: she tried the little golden key in the lock, and to her great delight it fitted!

Alice opened the door and found that it led into a small passage, not much larger than a rat-hole: she knelt down and looked along the passage into the loveliest garden you ever saw. How she longed to get out of that dark hall, and wander about among those beds of bright flowers and those cool fountains, but she could not even get her head though the doorway; "and even if my head would go through," thought poor Alice, "it would be of very little use without my shoulders. Oh, how I wish I could shut up like a telescope! I think I could, if I only knew how to begin." For, you see, so many out-of-the-way things had happened lately, that Alice had begun to think that very few things indeed were really impossible.

There seemed to be no use in waiting by the little door, so she went back to the table, half hoping she might find another key on it, or at any rate a book of rules for shutting people up like telescopes: this time she found a little bottle on it, ("which certainly was not here before," said Alice,) and round the neck of the bottle was a paper label, with the words "DRINK ME" beautifully printed on it in large letters.

It was all very well to say "Drink me," but the wise little Alice was not going to do that in a hurry. "No, I'll look first," she said, "and see whether it's marked 'poison' or not"; for she had read several nice little histories about children who had got burnt, and eaten up by wild beasts and other unpleasant things, all because they would not remember the simple rules their friends had taught them: such as, that a red-hot

poker will burn you if you hold it too long; and that if you cut your finger very deeply with a knife, it usually bleeds; and she had never forgotten that, if you drink much from a bottle marked "poison," it is almost certain to disagree with you, sooner or later.

However, this bottle was not marked "poison," so Alice ventured to taste it, and finding it very nice, (it had, in fact, a sort of mixed flavour of cherry-tart, custard, pine-apple, roast turkey, toffee, and hot buttered toast), she very soon finished it off.

"What a curious feeling!" said Alice; "I must be shutting up like a telescope."

  *   *   *   *   *   *   *

And so it was indeed: she was now only ten-inches high, and her face brightened up at the thought that she was now the right size for going through the little door into that lovely garden. First, however, she waited for a few minutes to see if she was going to shrink any further: she felt a little nervous about this; "for it might end, you know," said Alice to herself, "in my going out altogether, like a candle. I wonder what I should be like then?" And she tried to fancy what the flame of a candle is like after the candle is blown out, for she could not remember ever having seen such a thing.

After a while, finding that nothing more happened, she decided on going into the garden at once; but, alas for poor Alice! when she got to the door, she found she had forgotten the little golden key, and when she went back to the table for it, she found she could not possibly reach it: she could see it quite plainly through the glass, and she tried her best to climb up one of the legs of the table, but it was too slippery; and when

poker: a rod, usually of iron, for stirring a fire.

she had tired herself out with trying, the poor little thing sat down and cried.

"Come, there's no use in crying like that!" said Alice to herself, rather sharply; "I advise you to leave off this minute!" She generally gave herself very good advice (though she very seldom followed it), and sometimes she scolded herself so severely as to bring tears into her eyes; and once she remembered trying to box her own ears for having cheated herself in a game of croquet she was playing against herself, for this curious child was very fond of pretending to be two people. "But it's no use now," thought poor Alice, "to pretend to be two people! Why, there's hardly enough of me left to make *one* respectable person!"

Soon her eye fell on a little glass box that was lying under the table: she opened it, and found in it a very small cake, on which the words "EAT ME" were beautifully marked in **currants**.

"Well, I'll eat it," said Alice, "and if it makes me grow larger, I can reach the key; and if it makes me grow smaller, I can creep under the door; so either way I'll get into the garden, and I don't care which happens!"

She ate a little bit, and said anxiously to herself, "Which way? Which way?", holding her hand on the top of her head to feel which way it was growing, and she was quite surprised to find that she remained the same size: to be sure, this generally happens when one eats cake, but Alice had got so much into the way of expecting nothing but out-of-the-way things to happen, that it seemed quite dull and stupid for life to go on in the common way.

So she set to work, and very soon finished off the cake.

currants: the raisin of a small seedless grape grown in the Mediterranean region, used in cooking.

COMMENTARY

The story begins with an introductory poem that sets up the action that will follow. *Alice's Adventures in Wonderland* is inspired by several afternoons in 1862 when Lewis Carroll frequently went boating with the Liddell sisters, Lorina, Alice, and Edith, who, respectively, are referred to as Prima, Secunda, and Tertia in the poem. The three sisters ask the narrator to tell them a story, and he complies. Prima demands the narrator to "begin it;" Secunda requires that the narrator include elements of nonsense; and Tertia frequently interrupts the narrative.

By the fifth stanza, the poem reads as an apology for the narrator's limited imagination and story-telling ability. He claims that the effort of telling the story has "drained the wells of fancy dry." When he attempts to conclude the story at a later date, the young women request that he finish it now: "It is next time!" The narrator claims that these are the external events leading to the story that follows.

Chapter I begins with Alice sitting on a riverbank with her sister. The day is hot, and Alice is bored and feeling sleepy. Her sister reads a book. Alice tries to interest herself in her sister's book, but she soon turns away because it contains no pictures or conversations. Because words are abstract representations, Alice refuses to make the effort to connect the abstractions with more concrete pictures using her own imagination. Instead, she considers making a daisy chain, but she remains idle while wondering whether it would be worth the effort to collect daisies. At this point in the story, the reader assumes that Alice falls asleep and dreams the adventures that follow.

Alice spies a White Rabbit (in the story, creatures with human characteristics are referred to with a proper name). Seeing a rabbit in a field seems natural, but then Alice overhears the White Rabbit mutter, "Oh dear! Oh dear! I shall be too late!" The White Rabbit introduces the literary element of anthropomorphism (attributing human characteristics to an animal or inanimate object) into the story. The White Rabbit's human characteristics prepare the reader for the other anthropomorphized characters that appear later in the book.

The Rabbit is wearing a sport coat and vest from which he removes a watch. The Rabbit checks the time while moving hurriedly along. Carroll uses the skittish nature of the Rabbit to illustrate how neurotically some human individuals adhere to schedules. After all, Carroll himself related the story one quiet, lazy Friday afternoon in July, a direct contrast to the schedule obsession Carroll more than likely experienced during the school year.

Her curiosity piqued by the Rabbit wearing a vest and coat, Alice proceeds to follow the Rabbit across the field and watches him pop down a rabbit-hole under a hedge. Alice follows him into the hole, and moves along a tunnel until she suddenly falls downward. Carroll's background in mathematics comes into play in his description of this scene. During her fall, Alice is unable to calculate how far or how fast she is descending. The subterranean descent, moreover, reflects a philosophical and scientific fascination with the concept of a hole that would pass through the earth that was examined by, among others, Galileo and Francis Bacon. Among the questions considered by such individuals were changes in air pressure and gravity as one neared and passed through the center of the earth.

During a long, slow, and steady free-fall, Alice is able to examine the walls of the hole, which are lined with cupboards and shelves, pictures and maps. From a shelf she takes a jar labeled "ORANGE MARMALADE," finds it empty, and places it on another shelf. In this instance, Carroll has fun with labels humans grant objects. The jar in and of itself is only a jar. Placing a label on it that reads "ORANGE MARMALADE" might indicate that the object we call a jar contains a substance called marmalade. However, this jar contains nothing, rendering the label deceptive. The label would more accurately read "Empty."

In pursuit of the White Rabbit, Alice falls down a strange rabbit-hole.
Mary Evans Picture Library

Alice places the jar on a shelf because she fears she may drop it, but in this she contradicts the gravitational findings of Galileo and Sir Isaac Newton. Because she is falling herself, dropping the jar is an impossibility. The best she can do is simply let go her hold of the jar, because it would fall at the same speed as Alice.

Alice feels brave for having fallen so far, commenting to herself that this fall is further than if she had fallen off the top of her house. Alice attempts to say that a fall from the top of her house wouldn't be reason to boast compared to this fall, but instead she says that she wouldn't talk if she fell from the house. The story's narrator comments parenthetically on this statement by saying that no, she probably wouldn't speak—implying that she would be unable to speak because she'd be killed in such a fall. This type of dark humor appears throughout *Alice's Adventures in Wonderland*.

Alice believes that she has fallen for miles and miles and might reach the center of the earth. She remembers from school that the earth's center is 4,000 miles from the surface. She considers as well that she might fall past the center and on to the other side of the earth. She wonders what longitude and latitude she has reached, even though the narrator makes it obvious that she has no idea what either word signifies.

Alice imagines that she will emerge in a land where everything is upside down, perhaps in "The Antipathies." The name doesn't sound right to her, and is the first instance of a malapropism (misuse of words caused by similarity in sound) in *Alice's Adventures in Wonderland*. Alice is probably trying to say the Antipodes, which is what the English called Australia and New Zealand. However, the word "antipodes" also denotes that which is exactly the opposite. Carroll could be using the literary device of foreshadowing (indicating or suggesting something that is going to happen later in the story) to describe the illogical and irrational world of Wonderland, which is diametrically opposed to the rigid and staid world of Victorian England.

Alice prepares herself to inquire as to the name of the country where she ended up. "Please, Ma'am, is this New Zealand or Australia?" she imagines herself saying, and she practices curtseying, but curtseying proves very difficult while falling. Alice realizes, however, that she would be thought ignorant if she asked such a question as the name of the country in which she was standing. She hopes to find the location written down somewhere instead, indicating that Alice puts her faith in the written label or what an object or place is called rather than in her own instincts.

Still falling, and with nothing else to do, Alice begins to think of her life back home, and she also worries about her cat, Dinah. She hopes someone will set out milk for Dinah. She wishes Dinah was with her, but then she becomes concerned that there are no mice in the hole for Dinah to feed on. There might be bats in the air, Alice thinks, and then she wonders whether cats eat bats. Becoming sleepy, she repeats her question, but it becomes reversed in her drowsy state, as she considers whether bats eat cats, concluding that it doesn't matter either way. But her understanding of the question as an algebraic equation rather than a logical supposition is incorrect. In this instance, Alice equates the question as similar to: If $1 + 2 = 3$, then $2 + 1 = 3$, which is correct. But, in transposing the verbal equation of cats eating bats to bats eating cats, Alice is obviously in error. There is certainly a difference as to whether cats eat bats or vice versa. Her fall ends suddenly with a thump, as she lands on a heap of dry leaves and sticks.

Alice jumps to her feet, unharmed. There is darkness above her, and a passage spread out before her, where she spots the White Rabbit scurrying along. Alice gives chase and gets close enough to hear the Rabbit mutter, "Oh my ears and whiskers, how late it's getting," but when she turns a corner in pursuit, the Rabbit is no longer in sight.

Alice finds herself in a long, low hall with lights suspended from the ceiling and doors all around. After trying to open the doors and finding that they are all locked, Alice wanders sadly to the middle of the room where she finds a three-legged, glass table. On top of the table is a small golden key. Alice uses the key to try and open doors, but all of the locks on the doors are too large for the tiny key. Alice illogically reasons that the key she possesses is the correct key (which it may or may not be) and that either the locks are too large or the key is too small. She fails to take into consideration that the particular key she is using may not be correct for the particular door she is trying to unlock.

However, Alice discovers a small curtain she has not noticed before. She pulls back the curtain and finds a small door only fifteen inches high. The small key fits the door, and Alice opens it. She finds herself looking into the loveliest of gardens, with bright flowers and cool fountains. She wants to go there, but she cannot fit even her head through the small opening. She wishes that she could be a retractable telescope that could be shut into a small object. After the recent events she has experienced, she believes that few things are impossible.

Alice returns to the glass table, hoping to find another key or perhaps a book that explains how to fold-in like a telescope. Instead, she finds a small bottle with a paper label that reads "DRINK ME" in elegant lettering. After being careful to

Alice discovers a small door hidden behind a curtain.
Mary Evans Picture Library

make sure the bottle is not marked "poison," she drinks the liquid, which tastes of cherry-tart, custard, pineapple, roast turkey, toffee, and hot-buttered toast. Her faith that the liquid isn't poison rests solely on the fact that no label denotes whether the bottle's contents are safe or unsafe. This is similar to the jar marked "ORANGE MARMALADE," which, in fact, was not. Many critics speculate that the bottle contains laudanum, a mixture of opiates and alcohol widely available for public consumption in Victorian England. Alice's subsequent adventures certainly indicate that she might be suffering from the hallucinatory effects of a mind-altering substance. While her adventures thus far consist of a dreamlike quality, what follows resembles more of a hallucination.

Alice begins getting smaller, to the point where she is only ten-inches high. She is happy when she stops shrinking as she was afraid that she might disappear entirely, like the flame of a candle when it goes out (and she wonders what the flame looks like after it goes out). She is unconsciously questioning the nature of existence and the possibility of a life beyond the corporeal (physical or bodily) realm. She quickly abandons this philosophical questioning and reasons that her smaller state will enable her to fit through the small door and enter the lovely garden.

When she reaches the door, however, Alice realizes that she has forgotten the key. Returning to the table, she spots the key through the transparent glass tabletop on which the key is set. Being only ten inches tall, Alice cannot reach the key, and the glass legs of the table prove too slippery to climb. Dejected, Alice sits down on the floor and weeps.

Then, she scolds herself for crying. Usually, Alice is able to give herself good advice. One time, however, she scolded herself so severely that she began to cry. On another occasion, Alice boxes her own ears for cheating at croquet. She was playing against herself on that occasion. Alice is often fond of pretending to be two people. Now, however, in her reduced state of being ten-inches tall, "there's hardly enough of me," she remarks, "to make *one* respectable person." This reasoning, like most of Alice's postulations, is in error. She mistakes an individual's size for his or her individuality.

Alice notices a small glass box underneath the table. Inside the small box is a cake with the words "EAT ME" spelled out by currants. As she begins to eat the cake, Alice places her hand on her head to see if she is growing. As usual when eating cake, Alice remains the same size. However, she becomes so used to "out-of-the-way things" happening that she is surprised when nothing happens as she eats the cake. It seems "quite dull and stupid" to return to the common ways of life, she observes, presumptuously assuming that, by definition, always anticipating unexpected events negates their unexpectedness. The chapter ends as Alice finishes the rest of the cake, hoping for an out-of-the-way result.

Alice drinks the contents of a bottle labelled DRINK ME and shrinks to a height of ten inches.
Mary Evans Picture Library

Chapter II: The Pool of Tears

Alice grows more than nine-feet tall, frightens the White Rabbit, shrinks to the height of two-feet tall, and swims in a pool of her own tears with a Mouse.

[handwritten annotations: "now phrase used quite alot." "shows how Wonderland effects you."]

NOTES

"Curiouser and curiouser!" cried Alice (she was so much surprised, that for the moment she quite forgot how to speak good English); "now I'm opening out like the largest telescope that ever was! Good-bye, feet!" (for when she looked down at her feet, they seemed to be almost out of sight, they were getting so far off). "Oh, my poor little feet, I wonder who will put on your shoes and stockings for you now, dears? I'm sure *I* shan't be able! I shall be a great deal too far off to trouble myself about you: you must manage the best way you can — but I must be kind to them," thought Alice, "or perhaps they won't walk the way I want to go! Let me see: I'll give them a new pair of boots every Christmas." And she went on planning to herself how she would manage it. "They must go by the carrier," *[handwritten: "semantic change."]* she thought; "and how funny it'll seem, sending presents to one's own feet! And how odd the directions will look!

Alice's Right Foot, Esq.
Hearthrug,
near the Fender,
(with Alice's love).

"Oh dear, what nonsense I'm talking!"
Just then her head struck against the roof of the hall: in fact she was now more than nine feet high, and she at once took up the little golden key and hurried off to the garden door.
Poor Alice! It was as much as she could do, lying down on one side, to look through into the

Alice grows to more than nine-feet tall after ingesting a cake labelled "EAT ME."
Mary Evans Picture Library

garden with one eye; but to get through was more hopeless than ever: she sat down and began to cry again.

"You ought to be ashamed of yourself," said Alice, "a great girl like you," (she might well say this), "to go on crying in this way! Stop this moment, I tell you!" But she went on all the same, shedding gallons of tears, until there was a large pool all round her, about four inches deep and reaching half down the hall.

After a time she heard a little pattering of feet in the distance, and she hastily dried her eyes to see what was coming. It was the White Rabbit returning, splendidly dressed, with a pair of white **kid gloves** in one hand and a large fan in the other: he came trotting along in a great hurry, muttering to himself as he came, "Oh! the Duchess, the Duchess! Oh! won't she be savage if I've kept her waiting!" Alice felt so desperate that she was ready to ask help of any one; so, when the Rabbit came near her, she began, in a low, timid voice, "If you please, sir—" The Rabbit started violently, dropped the white kid gloves and the fan, and skurried away into the darkness as hard as he could go.

Alice took up the fan and gloves, and, as the hall was very hot, she kept fanning herself all the time she went on talking: "Dear, dear! How queer everything is to-day! And yesterday things went on just as usual. I wonder if I've been changed in the night? Let me think: was I the same when I got up this morning? I almost think I can remember feeling a little different. But if I'm not the same, the next question is, Who in the world am I? Ah, *that's* the great puzzle!" And she began thinking over all the children she knew that were of the same age as herself, to see if she could have been changed for any of them.

kid gloves: leather gloves made from the skin of young goats.

"I'm sure I'm not Ada," she said, "for her hair goes in such long ringlets, and mine doesn't go in ringlets at all; and I'm sure I can't be Mabel, for I know all sorts of things, and she, oh! she knows such a very little! Besides, *she's* she, and I'm I, and—oh dear, how puzzling it all is! I'll try if I know all the things I used to know. Let me see: four times five is twelve, and four times six is thirteen, and four times seven is—oh dear! I shall never get to twenty at that rate! However, the Multiplication Table doesn't signify: let's try Geography. London is the capital of Paris, and Paris is the capital of Rome, and Rome—no, *that's* all wrong, I'm certain! I must have been changed for Mabel! I'll try and say 'How doth the little—'" and she crossed her hands on her lap as if she were saying lessons, and began to repeat it, but her voice sounded hoarse and strange, and the words did not come the same as they used to do:

> 'How doth the little crocodile
>   Improve his shining tail,
> And pour the waters of the Nile
>   On every golden scale!
>
> 'How cheerfully he seems to grin,
>   How neatly spread his claws,
> And welcome little fishes in
>   With gently smiling jaws!

"I'm sure those are not the right words," said poor Alice, and her eyes filled with tears again as she went on, "I must be Mabel after all, and I shall have to go and live in that poky little house, and have next to no toys to play with, and oh! ever so many lessons to learn! No, I've made up my mind about it; if I'm Mabel, I'll stay down

[Handwritten margin notes: "questions society", "competitive.", "comparing everything to known situations", "all knowledge etc. but no teaching of real world.", "wonderland could be seen as reality?", "violence.", "Alice must be quite well off.", "snobby", "parody", "society: class system concerned with appearances + possessions."]

here! It'll be no use their putting their heads down and saying 'Come up again, dear!' I shall only look up and say 'Who am I then? Tell me that first, and then, if I like being that person, I'll come up: if not, I'll stay down here till I'm somebody else'—but, oh dear!" cried Alice, with a sudden burst of tears, "I do wish they *would* put their heads down! I am so *very* tired of being all alone here!"

As she said this she looked down at her hands, and was surprised to see that she had put on one of the Rabbit's little white kid gloves while she was talking. "How *can* I have done that?" she thought. "I must be growing small again." She got up and went to the table to measure herself by it, and found that, as nearly as she could guess, she was now about two feet high, and was going on shrinking rapidly: she soon found out that the cause of this was the fan she was holding, and she dropped it hastily, just in time to avoid shrinking away altogether.

"That *was* a narrow escape!" said Alice, a good deal frightened at the sudden change, but very glad to find herself still in existence; "and now for the garden!" and she ran with all speed back to the little door: but, alas! the little door was shut again, and the little golden key was lying on the glass table as before, "and things are worse than ever," thought the poor child, "for I never was so small as this before, never! And I declare it's too bad, that it is!"

As she said these words her foot slipped, and in another moment, splash! she was up to her chin in salt water. Her first idea was that she had somehow fallen into the sea, "and in that case I can go back by railway," she said to herself. (Alice had been to the seaside once in her life, and had come to the general conclusion, that

---

Handwritten margin notes:

Effect of Wonderland:
- confusion.
- sense of place.
- identity
- reasoning & logic. → still insists on being superior.
- language.
- metamorphosis
- sense / nonsense.
- physical
- growth & shrinking
- emotional
- mood swings
- acceptance.

nature of language: can't always say what we mean: only so many words.

class riddles, money driven.

wherever you go to on the English coast you find a number of bathing machines in the sea, some children digging in the sand with wooden spades, then a row of lodging houses, and behind them a railway station.) However, she soon made out that she was in the pool of tears which she had wept when she was nine feet high.

"I wish I hadn't cried so much!" said Alice, as she swam about, trying to find her way out. "I shall be punished for it now, I suppose, by being drowned in my own tears! That *will* be a queer thing, to be sure! However, everything is queer to-day."

Just then she heard something splashing about in the pool a little way off, and she swam nearer to make out what it was: at first she thought it must be a walrus or hippopotamus, but then she remembered how small she was now, and she soon made out that it was only a mouse that had slipped in like herself.

"Would it be of any use, now," thought Alice, "to speak to this mouse? Everything is so out-of-the-way down here, that I should think very likely it can talk: at any rate, there's no harm in trying." So she began: "O Mouse, do you know the way out of this pool? I am very tired of swimming about here, O Mouse!" (Alice thought this must be the right way of speaking to a mouse: she had never done such a thing before, but she remembered having seen in her brother's Latin Grammar, "A mouse—of a mouse—to a mouse—a mouse—O mouse!" The Mouse looked at her rather inquisitively, and seemed to her to wink with one of its little eyes, but it said nothing.

"Perhaps it doesn't understand English," thought Alice; "I daresay it's a French mouse, come over

Alice swims in a pool of her own tears.
Mary Evans Picture Library

with **William the Conqueror**." (For, with all her knowledge of history, Alice had no very clear notion how long ago anything had happened.) So she began again: **"Ou est ma chatte?"** which was the first sentence in her French lesson-book. The Mouse gave a sudden leap out of the water, and seemed to quiver all over with fright. "Oh, I beg your pardon!" cried Alice hastily, afraid that she had hurt the poor animal's feelings. "I quite forgot you didn't like cats."

"Not like cats!" cried the Mouse, in a shrill, passionate voice. "Would *you* like cats if you were me?"

"Well, perhaps not," said Alice in a soothing tone: "don't be angry about it. And yet I wish I could show you our cat Dinah: I think you'd take a fancy to cats if you could only see her. She is such a dear quiet thing," Alice went on, half to herself, as she swam lazily about in the pool, "and she sits purring so nicely by the fire, licking her paws and washing her face—and she is such a nice soft thing to nurse—and she's such a capital one for catching mice—oh, I beg your pardon!" cried Alice again, for this time the Mouse was bristling all over, and she felt certain it must be really offended. "We won't talk about her any more if you'd rather not."

"We indeed!" cried the Mouse, who was trembling down to the end of his tail. "As if I would talk on such a subject! Our family always *hated* cats: nasty, low, vulgar things! Don't let me hear the name again!"

"I won't indeed!" said Alice, in a great hurry to change the subject of conversation. "Are you— are you fond—of—of dogs?" The Mouse did not answer, so Alice went on eagerly: "There is such a nice little dog near our house I should like to

William the Conqueror: William I, 1027(?)–87; Duke of Normandy who invaded England and defeated Harold at the Battle of Hastings: King of England (1066–87).

Ou est ma chatte?: French for "Where is my cat?"

show you! A little bright-eyed **terrier**, you know, with oh, such long curly brown hair! And it'll fetch things when you throw them, and it'll sit up and beg for its dinner, and all sorts of things—I can't remember half of them—and it belongs to a farmer, you know, and he says it's so useful, it's worth a hundred pounds! He says it kills all the rats and—oh dear!" cried Alice in a sorrowful tone, "I'm afraid I've offended it again!" For the Mouse was swimming away from her as hard as it could go, and making quite a commotion in the pool as it went.

So she called softly after it, "Mouse dear! Do come back again, and we won't talk about cats or dogs either, if you don't like them!" When the Mouse heard this, it turned round and swam slowly back to her: its face was quite pale (with passion, Alice thought), and it said in a low trembling voice, "Let us get to the shore, and then I'll tell you my history, and you'll understand why it is I hate cats and dogs."

It was high time to go, for the pool was getting quite crowded with the birds and animals that had fallen into it: there were a Duck and a **Dodo**, a **Lory** and an Eaglet, and several other curious creatures. Alice led the way, and the whole party swam to the shore.

terrier: any member of several breeds of generally small and typically aggressive dogs, originally bred to rout vermin and small game animals from their lairs.

dodo: a large bird, now extinct, that had a hooked bill, short neck and legs, and rudimentary wings useless for flying: formerly found on Mauritius.

lory: any of several small, brightly colored, short-tailed parrots, native to Australia and the East Indies with a fringed, brushlike tip of the tongue for feeding on soft fruits and nectar.

COMMENTARY

Even as she exclaims that things are growing "curioser," Alice continues to grow larger. She grows so tall that she can hardly see her feet. She begins thinking of different ways she might treat her feet, because she can no longer see them. She decides to send them a pair of new boots every Christmas, a thought that some critics believe indicates the nature of colonial Victorian England; Alice's extremities are now colonies that she must bribe to retain their respective loyalties. The thought of sending gifts to one's own feet amuses her, and she imagines also including a card addressed to her feet. However, she realizes that sending gifts and cards to one's own feet is absurd, and declares, "Oh dear, what nonsense I'm talking!" Alice uses the word nonsense whenever she must reject a prospective action or idea. Furthermore, Alice may be correct in declaring the act of giving oneself a present nonsense, because, as the word denotes, a present must come from a second party.

Alice grows more than nine-feet tall and her head strikes the roof of the hall. She reaches down for the small golden key on the table and goes over to the little door and opens it, but she can barely maneuver herself to see through the small door. She begins to cry again. Even though she admonishes herself to stop, Alice keeps crying. She weeps gallons of tears that fall to the ground and create a puddle of water four inches deep. While the term "gallons" may indicate that Carroll is exercising hyperbole (deliberate and obvious exaggeration used for effect), the term "gallons" indeed becomes a foreshadowing of future events, as Alice and several animals are depicted as swimming in a veritable pool of Alice's own tears after Alice diminishes in size.

Alice grows more than nine-feet tall.
The Everett Collection

The patter of feet draws her attention and she begins drying her eyes. Alice again sees the White Rabbit, this time splendidly dressed in a long coat and carrying a large fan and a pair of white kidgloves. He mutters aloud about keeping the Duchess waiting.

Alice speaks to the Rabbit, but her voice is so booming that the Rabbit drops the gloves and fan in fright and runs off into the darkness. Alice reaches for the objects dropped by the White Rabbit. She fans herself while she considers "how queer everything is today!" She recalls feeling a little different when she woke up that morning, and now she wonders if she changed overnight. She begins to question her identity. "If I'm not the same," she asks herself, "the next question is, 'Who in the world am I?'" Nothing she has experienced previously prepares Alice for the sudden changes in environment and body size she endures. Lacking a contemporary point of reference, she begins to doubt that her previous grasp of her own identity was correct. She ponders who she is: "Ah, *that's* the great puzzle."

After thinking she might be one of her friends, Alice confirms that she is neither Mabel nor Ada. She tries to remember things that she has learned. First she tries using multiplication, but her answers are not correct ("the Multiplication-Table doesn't signify," she concludes). She tries geography, but she mixes up facts (she says that London is the capital of Paris, and Paris is the capital of Rome, for example). Finally, she tries to remember a verse lesson—a poem entitled "Against Idleness and Mischief" by Isaac Watts—but it becomes a parody about a crocodile. Some critics believe that this parody indicates Carroll's rebellious nature against his own restrictive upbringing. In any event, Alice is attempting to find a point of reference for the fantastic world she has entered by trying to apply generally accepted "facts" from her former world. These facts, however, do not apply in Wonderland, which increasingly frustrates Alice.

Determined to not leave the hole if she is someone else, Alice plans to ask "Who am I, then?" to people looking down the hole and pleading for her to return. If she does not like the person they name, Alice will remain in the hole until they name someone whom she wants to be. In this instance, Alice gives up trying to define who she is, and now looks to others to project their impressions as to her identity. Alice bursts into tears again; she wishes

that someone would appear because she is tired of being all alone.

Noticing that her hand is small enough to put inside one of the kid-gloves that the Rabbit had dropped, Alice discovers that she has been shrinking. As she diminishes in size, Alice realizes that the fan she is holding is causing the effect. She drops it before she becomes reduced to nothing, reminding the reader of the candle flame analogy in Chapter I, in which she pondered whether a flame exists after it is extinguished. Then, she runs to the small door that leads to the garden, but again she forgets to bring the key.

Alice walks dejectedly, having never been (or felt) so small before. Her foot slips and she falls into a pool of salt water. Thinking she has fallen into the sea and, therefore, that she can catch a train to return home (based on her only previous experience at the sea), Alice again exposes her habit of trying to apply previous experiences to new and unrelated events. Alice realizes that she is in a pool formed by the tears she cried when she was nine-feet tall. Wishing she hadn't cried so much, Alice becomes afraid that she might drown in her own tears. "That will be a queer thing, to be sure!" she notes. "However," she adds, "everything is queer today." By this, Alice rightly applies a revised logic according to her recent circumstances.

Hearing a splashing of water nearby, Alice swims over, thinking she might encounter a walrus or a hippopotamus. Alice is still applying a scale of reference from her experience prior to entering Wonderland. Instead of a walrus or hippo, however, she discovers a Mouse about the same size as she. Correctly thinking that everything is "so out-of-the-way down here," Alice finds no harm in trying to talk to the Mouse. She asks him for help in finding the way out of the pool, then, when he does not reply, she wonders about the correct way to address the Mouse.

Relying on her little knowledge of history, she considers that the Mouse might be French, having come to England with William the Conqueror. Alice, therefore, addresses him by using the first sentence she had learned from her French lesson book—"Où est ma chatte?" or, "Where is my cat?" The mention of a cat is frightening to a Mouse in any language. In this instance, the Mouse equates the word "chatte" with the actual physical presence of a cat, which is an absurd assumption to make.

Regardless, Alice quickly apologizes. She swims lazily while assuring the Mouse that he would like Dinah, Alice's cat. She begins noting Dinah's habits—sitting and purring by a fire, grooming herself, and so forth—but she has to apologize again when she mentions that Dinah catches mice. This is another instance of Carroll using dark humor. The Mouse is afraid of being eaten by a cat owned by a little girl no larger than he is, which indicates carnivorous behavior. Regardless, Alice is only aware of her past experience and is not able to adjust to her new size or surroundings with an appropriate sense of decorum.

"We won't talk about her anymore," assures Alice, to which the Mouse replies, while trembling, "As if *I* would talk on such a subject!" The Mouse adds that his family hates cats. Alice changes the subject to dogs and begins speaking of her neighbor's bright-eyed terrier. The terrier fetches things and begs for food, she says. However, when she again displays poor manners by describing the dog's talent for killing rats, the Mouse swims away.

Alice calls out to the Mouse, promising not to talk about cats or dogs. The Mouse returns and suggests they swim to the shore, where the Mouse will tell her a story to illustrate why he hates cats and dogs.

It is a good time to leave the pool because it is suddenly crowded. Alice and the Mouse are joined in their swim to shore by many birds and animals that have fallen into the pool, including a Dodo, a Duck, a Lory (a small, brightly colored parrot), and an Eaglet. Some readers regard the pool of tears as a primordial soup from which life emerges, according to the theory of evolution promoted by Charles Darwin scarcely a decade prior to Carroll's writing of *Alice's Adventures in Wonderland*.

Chapter III: A Caucus-Race and a Long Tale

Alice participates in the Caucus-race, mixes up a long sad tale with the tail of the Mouse, and scares off many birds by mentioning the skills of her cat, Dinah.

They were indeed a queer-looking party that assembled on the bank—the birds with **draggled** feathers, the animals with their fur clinging close to them, and all dripping wet, cross, and uncomfortable.

The first question of course was, how to get dry again: they had a consultation about this, and after a few minutes it seemed quite natural to Alice to find herself talking familiarly with them, as if she had known them all her life. Indeed, she had quite a long argument with the Lory, who at last turned sulky, and would only say, "I am older than you, and must know better"; and this Alice would not allow without knowing how old it was, and, as the Lory positively refused to tell its age, there was no more to be said.

At last the Mouse, who seemed to be a person of authority among them, called out, "Sit down, all of you, and listen to me! *I'll* soon make you dry enough!" They all sat down at once, in a large ring, with the Mouse in the middle. Alice kept her eyes anxiously fixed on it, for she felt sure she would catch a bad cold if she did not get dry very soon.

"Ahem!" said the Mouse with an important air, "are you all ready? This is the **driest** thing I know. Silence all round, if you please! 'William the Conqueror, whose cause was favoured by the pope, was soon submitted to by the English, who wanted leaders, and had been of late much accustomed to **usurpation** and conquest.

NOTES

draggled: made wet and dirty by dragging in mud or water.

driest: used as a pun on the double meaning of "dry," meaning to remove wetness as well as boring, dull, or tedious.

usurpation: the unlawful or violent seizure of a throne, power, and so forth.

understanding.

tea knowledge but not

Edwin and **Morcar**, the earls of **Mercia** and
Northumbria—'"

"Ugh!" said the Lory, with a shiver.

"I beg your pardon!" said the Mouse, frowning,
but very politely: "Did you speak?"

"Not I!" said the Lory hastily.

"I thought you did," said the Mouse. "—I proceed. 'Edwin and Morcar, the earls of Mercia and
Northumbria, declared for him: and even **Stigand**, the patriotic **archbishop of Canterbury**,
found it advisable—'"

"Found *what*?" said the Duck.

"Found *it*," the Mouse replied rather crossly: "of
course you know what 'it' means."

"I know what 'it' means well enough, when I
find a thing," said the Duck: "it's generally a frog
or a worm. The question is, what did the archbishop find?"

The Mouse did not notice this question, but
hurriedly went on, "'—found it advisable to go
with **Edgar Atheling** to meet William and offer
him the crown. William's conduct at first was
moderate. But the insolence of his **Normans**—'
How are you getting on now, my dear?" it continued, turning to Alice as it spoke.

"As wet as ever," said Alice in a melancholy tone:
"it doesn't seem to dry me at all."

"In that case," said the Dodo solemnly, rising to
its feet, "I move that the meeting **adjourn**, for
the immediate adoption of more energetic
remedies—'"

"Speak English!" said the Eaglet. "I don't know
the meaning of half those long words, and,
what's more, I don't believe you do either!" And
the Eaglet bent down its head to hide a smile:
some of the other birds tittered audibly.

*doesn't
stand.*

*Edwin the Earl of Mercia, Morcar the Earl of Northum-
bria, Stigand the Archbishop of Canterbury, Edgar
Atheling:* Early English historical figures.

Normans: any of the Scandanavians who occupied Normandy in the tenth century.

*superior because of long
words.*

adjourn: to put off or suspend until a future time.

difficulty of language.

"What I was going to say," said the Dodo in an offended tone, "was, that the best thing to get us dry would be a **Caucus**-race."

"What *is* a Caucus-race?" said Alice; not that she wanted much to know, but the Dodo had paused as if it thought that *somebody* ought to speak, and no one else seemed inclined to say anything.

"Why," said the Dodo, "the best way to explain it is to do it." (And, as you might like to try the thing yourself, some winter day, I will tell you how the Dodo managed it.)

First it marked out a race-course, in a sort of circle, ("the exact shape doesn't matter," it said,) and then all the party were placed along the course, here and there. There was no "One, two, three, and away," but they began running when they liked, and left off when they liked, so that it was not easy to know when the race was over. However, when they had been running half an hour or so, and were quite dry again, the Dodo suddenly called out "The race is over!" and they all crowded round it, panting, and asking, "But who has won?"

This question the Dodo could not answer without a great deal of thought, and it sat for a long time with one finger pressed upon its forehead (the position in which you usually see **Shakespeare**, in the pictures of him), while the rest waited in silence. At last the Dodo said, "*Everybody* has won, and all must have prizes."

"But who is to give the prizes?" quite a chorus of voices asked.

"Why, *she*, of course," said the Dodo, pointing to Alice with one finger; and the whole party at once crowded round her, calling out in a confused way, "Prizes! Prizes!"

Alice had no idea what to do, and in despair she put her hand in her pocket, and pulled out a box

caucus: a private meeting of leaders or a committee of a political party or faction to decide on policy, pick candidates, and so forth, especially prior to a general, open meeting.

[handwritten note] Native American. in origin. suggests stupidity & futility politics.

[handwritten note] illogical

[handwritten note] like kids being grown up.

Shakespeare: William Shakespeare (1564–1616), English Renaissance poet and dramatist.

of **comfits**, (luckily the salt water had not got into it), and handed them round as prizes. There was exactly one a-piece all round.

"But she must have a prize herself, you know," said the Mouse.

"Of course," the Dodo replied very gravely. "What else have you got in your pocket?" he went on, turning to Alice.

"Only a **thimble**," said Alice sadly.

"Hand it over here," said the Dodo.

Then they all crowded round her once more, while the Dodo solemnly presented the thimble, saying "We beg your acceptance of this elegant thimble"; and, when it had finished this short speech, they all cheered.

Alice thought the whole thing very absurd, but they all looked so grave that she did not dare to laugh; and, as she could not think of anything to say, she simply bowed, and took the thimble, looking as solemn as she could.

The next thing was to eat the comfits: this caused some noise and confusion, as the large birds complained that they could not taste theirs, and the small ones choked and had to be patted on the back. However, it was over at last, and they sat down again in a ring, and begged the Mouse to tell them something more.

"You promised to tell me your history, you know," said Alice, "and why it is you hate—C and D," she added in a whisper, half afraid that it would be offended again.

"Mine is a long and a sad tale!" said the Mouse, turning to Alice, and sighing.

"It *is* a long tail, certainly," said Alice, looking down with wonder at the Mouse's tail; "but why do you call it sad?" And she kept on puzzling about it while the Mouse was speaking, so that her idea of the tale was something like this:—

comfits: a candy or sweetmeat; especially, a candied fruit, nut, and so forth.

thimble: a small cap worn as protection on the finger that pushes the needle in sewing.

homophones.

"Fury said to
a mouse, That
he met in the
house, "Let
us both go
to law: *I*
will prose-
cute *you.* —
Come, I'll
take no de-
nial: We
must have
the trial:
For really
this morn-
ing I've
nothing
to do."
Said the
mouse to
the cur,
"Such a
trial dear
sir, with
no jury
or judge,
would
be wast-
ing our
breath."
"I'll be
judge,
I'll be
jury,"
said
cun-
ning
old
Fury:
"I'll
try
the
whole
cause,
and
con-
demn
you to
death""

legal system doesn't like.

mouse hasn't done anything wrong. :)

violence.

"You are not **attending**!" said the Mouse to Alice
severely. "What are you thinking of?"
"I beg your pardon," said Alice very humbly:
"you had got to the fifth bend, I think?"
"I had not!" cried the Mouse, sharply and very
angrily.

homophone.

"A knot!" said Alice, always ready to make herself
useful, and looking anxiously about her. "Oh, do
let me help to undo it!"
"I shall do nothing of the sort," said the Mouse,
getting up and walking away. "You insult me by
talking such nonsense!"
"I didn't mean it!" pleaded poor Alice. "But
you're so easily offended, you know!"
The Mouse only growled in reply.
"Please come back and finish your story!" Alice
called after it; and the others all joined in chorus,
"Yes, please do!" but the Mouse only shook its
head impatiently, and walked a little quicker.
"What a pity it wouldn't stay!" sighed the Lory,
as soon as it was quite out of sight; and an old
Crab took the opportunity of saying to her
daughter "Ah, my dear! Let this be a lesson to
you never to lose *your* temper!" "Hold your
tongue, Ma!" said the young Crab, a little snap-
pishly. "You're enough to try the patience of an
oyster!"

play on language.

idiom.

roles of mother & daughter twisted.

"I wish I had our Dinah here, I know I do!" said
Alice aloud, addressing nobody in particular.
"She'd soon fetch it back!"
"And who is Dinah, if I might venture to ask the
question?" said the Lory.
Alice replied eagerly, for she was always ready to
talk about her pet: "Dinah's our cat. And she's
such a capital one for catching mice you can't
think! And oh, I wish you could see her after the
birds! Why, she'll eat a little bird as soon as look
at it!"

childish

old slang.

attending: [archaic] to pay attention, give heed.

This speech caused a remarkable sensation among the party. Some of the birds hurried off at once: one old **Magpie** began wrapping itself up very carefully, remarking, "I really must be getting home; the night-air doesn't suit my throat!" and a Canary called out in a trembling voice to its children, "Come away, my dears! It's high time you were all in bed!" On various pretexts they all moved off, and Alice was soon left alone. "I wish I hadn't mentioned Dinah!" she said to herself in a melancholy tone. "Nobody seems to like her, down here, and I'm sure she's the best cat in the world! Oh, my dear Dinah! I wonder if I shall ever see you any more!" And here poor Alice began to cry again, for she felt very lonely and low-spirited. In a little while, however, she again heard a little pattering of footsteps in the distance, and she looked up eagerly, half hoping that the Mouse had changed his mind, and was coming back to finish his story.

[handwritten marginal note:] → a bit insensitive to other people.

[handwritten marginal note:] → moodswings.

magpie: any of several jaylike corids, passerine birds characterized by black-and-white coloring, a long, tapering tail, and a habit of noisy chattering.

COMMENTARY

When the party of beasts, birds, and Alice reaches the shore all are wet and uncomfortable, they engage in a discussion about how to get dry. Alice feels comfortable talking to the animals, but she and the Lory (a small, brightly colored parrot) get into an argument. The Lory assumes that because he is older than Alice is, he has more knowledge. Alice disagrees, especially because the Lory does not reveal his age. The implication that age inherently transports wisdom or knowledge is an appeal for authority that does not necessarily exist. Whether or not the Lory or Alice is older is inconsequential in the long run, because age does not automatically impart experience or intelligence.

The Mouse takes command of the situation, demanding that everyone sit down. He claims that he can make everyone dry by telling a story. This pun on the word dry—which can mean both "unwet" as well as "dull"—reveals the unreliability of language to convey precisely what the speaker intends; therein lies the humor.

Alice listens attentively to the Mouse, fearing she will catch a cold if she doesn't dry off (become unwet) soon. The Mouse launches into a historical account of an incident involving William the Conqueror, the Pope, and two earls. This passage is excerpted from Haviland Chepmell's *Short Course of History*.

The Mouse is interrupted, first by the Lory, then by the Duck. Regarding Chepmell's phrase "found it advisable," the Duck challenges the Mouse on his use of the word "it"—the Duck believes that the word is generally used as a noun, while the Mouse has used "it" to refer to a circumstance. The Mouse has said that Stigand, archbishop of Canterbury, "found it advisable." The Duck argues that when he uses "it," he means he has found a frog or a worm. "What did the archbishop find?" he asks the Mouse. Again, Carroll is pointing out that language is only useful insofar as both the speaker and the audience agree on what a word signifies; such a generic pronoun as "it" conveys a significantly different connotation depending on how the listener receives the word.

Ignoring the Duck's question, the Mouse continues his story, but stops to ask Alice how she is getting on. When Alice replies that the story isn't helping her dry, the Dodo rises solemnly to suggest in formal language that the meeting should be stopped in favor of using other ways to dry off. The Eaglet complains that the Dodo's words are too long. The Eaglet also asserts that he doesn't know the meaning of the words employed by the Dodo and, further, that he doesn't believe the Dodo does either. Though offended, the Dodo continues, using more pedestrian language that can be easily understood by all present. The Dodo, however, suggests the group participate in a Caucus-race. The Dodo seems to be perpetually in a state of explaining what he means, moving from the abstract, Latin-derived words of his first speech to a more accessible, Anglo-Saxon vocabulary. In his overblown language, the Dodo seems to represent that the way in which an individual expresses him or herself grants that person authority, rather than what he or she actually intends to say.

When Alice asks for an explanation of a Caucus-race, the Dodo's grasp of public speaking fails him. The Dodo finds himself at a loss for description, which results in his reply that the best way to learn about something is to do it. The companions establish a not-quite circular racecourse ("the exact shape doesn't matter," the Dodo assures her), and the participants start at various points. They begin running without an official start and stop and restart whenever they want. Telling who won the race is difficult, but after a half-hour, when they are all dry, the Dodo declares that the race is over.

Asked who won the race, the Dodo pauses and thinks for a long while with a finger pressed to his head. Finally, he exclaims that everybody has won, and all must receive prizes. This statement represents an inflation of language to create a false sense of fairness. Logically, no one can win if no one loses.

When asked who will give the prizes, the Dodo points to Alice. Everyone crowds around Alice calling for a prize. Alice is at a loss about what to do, but in her pocket she finds a box of comfits (mints). She has enough mints for everyone but herself. She also finds a thimble in her pocket. The Dodo takes the thimble. After a short, solemn speech, the Dodo awards the thimble to Alice. She wants to laugh at the seriousness of the ceremony, but because everyone is solemn, she accepts the thimble with a humble bow. Alice has been made a fool by accepting as a "prize" something she already possessed. Of course, there is some consistent logic in awarding a prize for a contest in which all contestants are declared winners. Because Alice provides all the prizes, only she can supply her own prize. Because she has a limited number of mints, she is awarded her own thimble.

her comment, the Mouse continues his tale. The Mouse's tale is presented on the page in a thin, sinuous form that looks like a tail and grows thinner as it grows longer.

The tale concerns an individual named Fury who convinces a mouse to conduct a trial in which Fury will prosecute the mouse. Fury says he has nothing to do, and responds to the mouse's protests that they don't have enough individuals to judge the trial and render a verdict. Fury responds that he'll be prosecutor, judge, and jury, and concludes that he'll condemn the mouse to death. At first glance, the poem seems to resemble a cat playing with a captured mouse. Carroll, however, may have also used this as a metaphor (a figure of speech containing an implied comparison) for the legal system of Victorian England, where capital punishment in the form of public executions was still widely practiced.

The difference between the Mouse's presentation of his tale and Alice's focus on "tail" becomes too much for the Mouse. He accuses her of not paying attention. Alice, misunderstanding "not" for its homonym "knot," replies that the tail (or tale) is getting caught in a knot, and she offers to help undo it. Offended at having his tale interrupted and misunderstood, the Mouse walks away. "You insult me by talking such nonsense!" he says to Alice.

Alice pleads for the Mouse to return, and all the others join her in the request, but the Mouse does not return. The Lory remarks that it is a pity that the Mouse wouldn't stay. Alice wishes aloud for her cat Dinah, because she says Dinah would soon fetch the Mouse and return it. Asked about Dinah by the Lory, Alice explains that Dinah is a cat who catches mice and is also adept at catching and eating birds. Once again, Alice violates the decorum of Wonderland by discussing carnivorous

Alice, along with the party of beasts and birds, askes the Dodo to identify the winner of the Caucus-race.
Mary Evans Picture Library

Everyone begins eating their comfit, but many of them complain. The larger birds cannot taste their comfits, and small birds cannot swallow theirs. After they all calm down, everyone begs the Mouse to tell them more of his story. Alice reminds the Mouse that he promised to tell her why he hates "C and D" (a reference to cats and dogs).

The Mouse begins what he calls "a long sad tale." In one of many homonyms that occur throughout *Alice's Adventures in Wonderland*, Alice mistakes the word "tale" for its homonym "tail." She remarks that, indeed, the Mouse's tail is long, but she wonders why he calls it sad. Oblivious to behavior among an audience that would be her cat's prey. The result of this for Carroll's audience may be alternately horrifying (if the reader is sensitive to all living creatures) or humorous (if the reader sees it as simply another aspect of Carroll's penchant for morbid humor).

The remark about Dinah's bird-catching ability and Alice's assertion that Dinah will "eat a little bird as soon as look at it" causes quite a stir. All the birds become agitated: Some hurry off, and others begin making excuses to leave. A canary, for example, tells her children that bedtime has arrived, even though Carroll never depicts a nocturnal setting.

Alice wishes she hadn't mentioned Dinah's name again. She is sure that everyone would like Dinah, and realizes that she misses her cat. She begins to cry again, feeling lonely and low-spirited. As the chapter ends, she hears the pattering of feet and looks up, "half hoping" to see the Mouse returning to finish his story.

Chapter IV: The Rabbit Sends in a Little Bill

— pun on bill.

Inside the White Rabbit's house Alice grows so large she can't get out, survives attempts to free her, shrinks back to a smaller size, and escapes a mob of angry animals as well as a large and overly playful puppy.

NOTES

It was the White Rabbit, trotting slowly back again, and looking anxiously about as it went, as if it had lost something; and she heard it muttering to itself, "The Duchess! The Duchess! Oh my dear paws! Oh my fur and whiskers! She'll get me executed, as sure as **ferrets** are ferrets! Where *can* I have dropped them, I wonder?" Alice guessed in a moment that it was looking for the fan and the pair of white kid gloves, and she very good-naturedly began hunting about for them, but they were nowhere to be seen—everything seemed to have changed since her swim in the pool, and the great hall, with the glass table and the little door, had vanished completely.

twisted parody: humour.

violence

ferret: a small, domesticated polecat with pink eyes and yellowish fur, easily tamed for hunting rabbits, rats, and so forth.

inexplicably constantly changing

Very soon the Rabbit noticed Alice, as she went hunting about, and called out to her in an angry tone, "Why, Mary Ann, what *are* you doing out here? Run home this moment, and fetch me a pair of gloves and a fan! Quick, now!" And Alice was so much frightened that she ran off at once in the direction it pointed to, without trying to explain the mistake it had made.

"He took me for his housemaid," she said to herself as she ran. "How surprised he'll be when he finds out who I am! But I'd better take him his fan and gloves—that is, if I can find them." As she said this, she came upon a neat little house, on the door of which was a bright brass plate with the name "W. RABBIT" engraved upon it. She went in without knocking, and hurried upstairs, in great fear lest she should meet the real **Mary Ann**, and be turned out of the house before she had found the fan and gloves.

→ mistaken identity

→ forgetting her manners

Mary Ann: The White Rabbit's maid.

rical change.

getting lazier with language.

"How queer it seems," Alice said to herself, "to be going messages for a rabbit! I suppose Dinah'll be sending me on messages next!" And she began fancying the sort of thing that would happen: "'Miss Alice! Come here directly, and get ready for your walk!' 'Coming in a minute, nurse! But I've got to see that the mouse doesn't get out.' Only I don't think," Alice went on, "that they'd let Dinah stop in the house if it began ordering people about like that!"

By this time she had found her way into a tidy little room with a table in the window, and on it (as she had hoped) a fan and two or three pairs of tiny white kid gloves: she took up the fan and a pair of the gloves, and was just going to leave the room, when her eye fell upon a little bottle that stood near the looking-glass. There was no label this time with the words "DRINK ME," but nevertheless she uncorked it and put it to her lips. "I know *something* interesting is sure to happen," she said to herself, "whenever I eat or drink anything; so I'll just see what this bottle does. I do hope it'll make me grow large again, for really I'm quite tired of being such a tiny little thing!"

less cautious. Spontaneous. hot headed impulsive.

there are some authorities in Wonderland

It did so indeed, and much sooner than she had expected: before she had drunk half the bottle, she found her head pressing against the ceiling, and had to stoop to save her neck from being broken. She hastily put down the bottle, saying to herself, "That's quite enough—I hope I shan't grow any more—As it is, I can't get out at the door—I do wish I hadn't drunk quite so much!"

violence.

but not too bad because of humour.

Alas! it was too late to wish that! She went on growing, and growing, and very soon had to kneel down on the floor: in another minute there was not even room for this, and she tried the effect of lying down with one elbow against the door, and the other arm curled round her head.

Still she went on growing, and, as a last resource, she put one arm out of the window, and one foot up the chimney, and said to herself, "Now I can do no more, whatever happens. What *will* become of me?"

Luckily for Alice, the little magic bottle had now had its full effect, and she grew no larger: still it was very uncomfortable, and, as there seemed to be no sort of chance of her ever getting out of the room again, no wonder she felt unhappy.

"It was much pleasanter at home," thought poor Alice, "when one wasn't always growing larger and smaller, and being ordered about by mice and rabbits. I almost wish I hadn't gone down that rabbit-hole—and yet—and yet—it's rather curious, you know, this sort of life! I do wonder what *can* have happened to me! When I used to read fairy-tales, I fancied that kind of thing never happened, and now here I am in the middle of one! There ought to be a book written about me, that there ought! And when I grow up, I'll write one—but I'm grown up now," she added in a sorrowful tone; "at least there's no room to grow up any more *here*."

"But then," thought Alice, "shall I *never* get any older than I am now? That'll be a comfort, one way—never to be an old woman—but then—always to have lessons to learn! Oh, I shouldn't like *that!*" → *learning should be fun: but they're not.*

"Oh, you foolish Alice!" she answered herself. "How can you learn lessons in here? Why, there's hardly room for *you*, and no room at all for any lesson-books!"

And so she went on, taking first one side and then the other, and making quite a conversation of it altogether; but after a few minutes she heard a voice outside, and stopped to listen.

[handwritten margin note: weight + size : authority.]

"Mary Ann! Mary Ann!" said the voice. "Fetch me my gloves this moment!" Then came a little pattering of feet on the stairs. Alice knew it was the Rabbit coming to look for her, and she trembled till she shook the house, quite forgetting that she was now about a thousand times as large as the Rabbit, and had no reason to be afraid of it.

[handwritten margin note: afraid on authority figures.]

Presently the Rabbit came up to the door, and tried to open it; but, as the door opened inwards, and Alice's elbow was pressed hard against it, that attempt proved a failure. Alice heard it say to itself "Then I'll go round and get in at the window."

"*That* you won't" thought Alice, and, after waiting till she fancied she heard the Rabbit just under the window, she suddenly spread out her hand, and made a snatch in the air. She did not get hold of anything, but she heard a little shriek and a fall, and a crash of broken glass, from which she concluded that it was just possible it had fallen into a **cucumber-frame**, or something of the sort.

The White Rabbit avoids Alice's grasp.
Mary Evans Picture Library

[handwritten margin note: violence.]

cucumber-frame: a wooden garden construction used to contain the vines of a cucumber plant.

Next came an angry voice—the Rabbit's—"Pat! Pat! Where are you?" And then a voice she had never heard before, "Sure then I'm here! Digging for apples, yer honour!"

[handwritten margin note: illogical. (uneducated)]

"Digging for apples, indeed!" said the Rabbit angrily. "Here! Come and help me out of *this*!" (Sounds of more broken glass.)

"Now tell me, Pat, what's that in the window?"

"Sure, it's an arm, yer honour!" (He pronounced it "arrum.")

[handwritten margin note: class. servant. different dialect.]

"An arm, you goose! Who ever saw one that size? Why, it fills the whole window!"

"Sure, it does, yer honour: but it's an arm for all that."

"Well, it's got no business there, at any rate: go and take it away!"

→ dismissive.

There was a long silence after this, and Alice could only hear whispers now and then; such as, "Sure, I don't like it, yer honour, at all, at all!" "Do as I tell you, you coward!" and at last she spread out her hand again, and made another snatch in the air. This time there were *two* little shrieks, and more sounds of broken glass. "What a number of cucumber-frames there must be!" thought Alice. "I wonder what they'll do next! As for pulling me out of the window, I only wish they *could*! I'm sure I don't want to stay in here any longer!"

She waited for some time without hearing anything more: at last came a rumbling of little cart-wheels, and the sound of a good many voices all talking together: she made out the words: "Where's the other ladder?—Why, I hadn't to bring but one; Bill's got the other—Bill! fetch it here, lad!—Here, put 'em up at this corner—No, tie 'em together first—they don't reach half high enough yet—Oh! they'll do well enough; don't be particular—Here, Bill! catch hold of this rope—Will the roof bear?—Mind that loose **slate**—Oh, it's coming down! Heads below!" (a loud crash) — "Now, who did that?—It was Bill, I fancy—Who's to go down the chimney?—Nay, I shan't! *You* do it!—That I won't, then!—Bill's to go down—Here, Bill! the master says you're to go down the chimney!"

→ hyphens: broken conversation; commotion

"Oh! So Bill's got to come down the chimney, has he?" said Alice to herself. "Why, they seem to put everything upon Bill! I wouldn't be in Bill's place for a good deal: this fireplace is narrow, to be sure; but I *think* I can kick a little!"

She drew her foot as far down the chimney as she could, and waited till she heard a little

slate: a hard, fine-grained, metamorphic rock, usually formed from shale, that cleaves naturally into thin, smooth-surfaced layers, used as a roofing tile.

animal (she couldn't guess of what sort it was) scratching and scrambling about in the chimney close above her: then, saying to herself, "This is Bill," she gave one sharp kick, and waited to see what would happen next.

→ violence.

The first thing she heard was a general chorus of "There goes Bill!" then the Rabbit's voice along—"Catch him, you by the hedge!" then silence, and then another confusion of voices— "Hold up his head—Brandy now—Don't choke him—How was it, old fellow? What happened to you? Tell us all about it!"

Last came a little feeble, squeaking voice, ("That's Bill," thought Alice,) "Well, I hardly know—No more, thank ye; I'm better now—but I'm a deal too flustered to tell you—all I know is, something comes at me like a Jack-in-the-box, and up I goes like a sky-rocket!"

"So you did, old fellow!" said the others.

"We must burn the house down!" said the Rabbit's voice; and Alice called out as loud as she could, "If you do. I'll set Dinah at you!"

There was a dead silence instantly, and Alice thought to herself, "I wonder what they *will* do next! If they had any sense, they'd take the roof off." After a minute or two, they began moving about again, and Alice heard the Rabbit say, "A **barrowful** will do, to begin with."

barrowful: a wheelbarrow load.

"A barrowful of *what?*" thought Alice; but she had not long to doubt, for the next moment a shower of little pebbles came rattling in at the window, and some of them hit her in the face. "I'll put a stop to this," she said to herself, and shouted out, "You'd better not do that again!" which produced another dead silence.

Alice noticed with some surprise that the pebbles were all turning into little cakes as they lay on the floor, and a bright idea came into her head.

] magic.

"If I eat one of these cakes," she thought, "it's sure to make *some* change in my size; and as it can't possibly make me larger, it must make me smaller, I suppose."

So she swallowed one of the cakes, and was delighted to find that she began shrinking directly. As soon as she was small enough to get through the door, she ran out of the house, and found quite a crowd of little animals and birds waiting outside. The poor little Lizard, Bill, was in the middle, being held up by two guinea-pigs, who were giving it something out of a bottle. They all made a rush at Alice the moment she appeared; but she ran off as hard as she could, and soon found herself safe in a thick wood.

"The first thing I've got to do," said Alice to herself, as she wandered about in the wood, "is to grow to my right size again; and the second thing is to find my way into that lovely garden. I think that will be the best plan."

It sounded an excellent plan, no doubt, and very neatly and simply arranged; the only difficulty was, that she had not the smallest idea how to set about it; and while she was peering about anxiously among the trees, a little sharp bark just over her head made her look up in a great hurry. An enormous puppy was looking down at her with large round eyes, and feebly stretching out one paw, trying to touch her. "Poor little thing!" said Alice, in a coaxing tone, and she tried hard to whistle to it; but she was terribly frightened all the time at the thought that it might be hungry, in which case it would be very likely to eat her up in spite of all her coaxing.

Hardly knowing what she did, she picked up a little bit of stick, and held it out to the puppy; whereupon the puppy jumped into the air off all its feet at once, with a yelp of delight, and

[handwritten margin notes: "certainty of Wonderland. Illogical logic." / "acting on impulse again" / "violence."]

rushed at the stick, and made believe to worry it; then Alice dodged behind a great **thistle**, to keep herself from being run over; and the moment she appeared on the other side, the puppy made another rush at the stick, and tumbled head over heels in its hurry to get hold of it; then Alice, thinking it was very like having a game of play with a cart-horse, and expecting every moment to be trampled under its feet, ran round the thistle again; then the puppy began a series of short charges at the stick, running a very little way forwards each time and a long way back, and barking hoarsely all the while, till at last it sat down a good way off, panting, with its tongue hanging out of its mouth, and its great eyes half shut. This seemed to Alice a good opportunity for making her escape; so she set off at once, and ran till she was quite tired and out of breath, and till the puppy's bark sounded quite faint in the distance. "And yet what a dear little puppy it was!" said Alice, as she leant against a buttercup to rest herself, and fanned herself with one of the leaves: "I should have liked teaching it tricks very much, if—if I'd only been the right size to do it! Oh dear! I'd nearly forgotten that I've got to grow up again! Let me see—how IS it to be managed? I suppose I ought to eat or drink something or other; but the great question is, what?"

The great question certainly was, what? Alice looked all round her at the flowers and the blades of grass, but she did not see anything that looked like the right thing to eat or drink under the circumstances. There was a large mushroom growing near her, about the same height as herself; and when she had looked under it, and on both sides of it, and behind it, it occurred to her that she might as well look and see what was on the top of it.

thistle: any of various plants of the composite family, with prickly leaves and heads of white, purple, pink, or yellow flowers.

← authority again.
physical disadvantag[e]

She stretched herself up on tiptoe, and peeped over the edge of the mushroom, and her eyes immediately met those of a large caterpillar, that was sitting on the top with its arms folded, quietly smoking a long **hookah**, and taking not the smallest notice of her or of anything else.

hookah: a kind of water pipe associated with the Middle East, with a long flexible tube for drawing the smoke through water in a vase or bowl and cooling it.

COMMENTARY

The White Rabbit reenters: he is trotting about slowly and anxiously looking for the gloves and fan he had dropped earlier. He is still muttering about being late to see the Duchess. He exclaims that the Duchess will cause great harm to him if he is late. The White Rabbit's perceived threat from the Duchess also foreshadows the violent nature the Duchess will display later.

Alice starts searching for the gloves and fan as well. Since she left the pool, however, the scene has changed. The hall of doors and the glass table have vanished.

The Rabbit notices Alice hunting about and calls to her angrily, "Why, Mary Ann, what *are* you doing out here?" He tells her to run home and fetch a pair of gloves and a fan for him. Frightened by his tone, Alice runs off in the direction the Rabbit had pointed to as home.

Alice believes she has been mistaken for the White Rabbit's housemaid. She soon comes to a house with a bright brass plate on the door that reads "W. Rabbit." She enters the house and hurries upstairs. She considers how queer it is that she is running errands for a Rabbit, and fancies what would happen if her cat, Dinah, ordered her about. In this speculation, Alice is making half assumptions based upon the two realities with which she has become familiar. In the first reality exists her cat, Dinah. In the second reality, talking and officious animal characters exist, which Alice has begun to accept as a matter of course. She transposes the second reality upon the first by imagining Dinah behaving as imperiously as the White Rabbit. However, if Dinah were to behave that way in front of Alice's family, Alice believes her family would never let the cat in their house.

Alice enters a room and quickly finds a fan and several pairs of gloves. She is about to leave the room when she notices a little bottle near a looking glass. The bottle is not labeled, but Alice proceeds to drink from it. Tired of being small, she hopes the liquid in the bottle will make her large. Indeed, it does, but Alice really has no basis for assuming it will. She is still acting on impulse, not experience, and the consequences bear this out. Before drinking half the liquid in the bottle, Alice grows so large that she has to sit down on the floor to avoid having her head smash against the ceiling. To fit inside the room, she puts one arm through an open window and places one of her feet inside the opening of a fireplace.

By the time Alice stops growing, she fills the room and has no way of getting out. She begins to long for home, where she wasn't always growing larger and smaller or being ordered around by animals. Comparing her curious experiences to those recounted in fairy tales, she promises herself to write about them when she grows up. This pronouncement, coming from a fictional character unaware of her construct, is an amusing element later developed more fully by such postmodern writers as Paul Auster, whose novel *City of Glass* displays many affinities with the works of Carroll.

However, declaring that she plans to write about her experiences when she grows up forces Alice to realize that she is "grown up." She is a big girl after having drunk from the bottle, only she is not any older. In her failed reasoning, Alice mistakes size with the wisdom of a mature adult. She finds comfort by thinking she will never grow old, but she also realizes that always being young means she will have to do lessons each day for the rest of her life.

Alice continues considering the advantages and disadvantages of having grown so large. She will have to continue her lessons, but then she wonders how that will be possible when nothing else will fit in the room with her. When she hears a voice calling for Mary Ann, she stops thinking about herself. Martin Gardiner, in *The Annotated Alice* (W. W. Norton & Company, 2000), notes that the name "Mary Ann" may not be a literary convenience for Carroll inasmuch as it refers to the slang expression for the French guillotine used for beheading its victims. The reader will see how beheading becomes a broad theme later in *Alice's Adventures in Wonderland*.

Alice fears the White Rabbit is coming to look for her. The White Rabbit tries to push open the door, but Alice's elbow blocks it. After overhearing the Rabbit planning to go outside and enter the house through a window, Alice waits until she is sure the Rabbit is outside, and then she snatches at where she thinks he would be. She doesn't catch him, but she hears a shriek and the sound of broken glass.

The White Rabbit calls for someone named Pat, and someone replies that they are "Digging for apples, yer honor!" While seemingly nonsensical to dig for apples, Pat's Irish brogue indicates that he might be using an Irish slang expression, "Irish apples," for potatoes. Carroll never names what animal Pat might be, although the White Rabbit refers to him as a "silly goose" and Gardiner (W. W. Norton & Company, 2000) postulates that he might be a guinea pig. Unfortunately, John Tenniel did not provide an illustration to resolve the question. After more sounds of broken glass, Pat identifies the big thing sticking out of the window as an arm. The White Rabbit doesn't believe an arm could grow to that size. He orders Pat to remove the object sticking out of the window.

Alice makes another grab and catches nothing, but she hears two shrieks and more broken glass. Then she hears the sounds of the wheels of a cart and several voices. From the voices she understands that a ladder has been put up on the side of the house and someone named Bill is climbing to the roof and planning to enter down the chimney. Waiting until she hears sounds in the chimney, Alice uses her foot inside the fireplace to kick upward. She punts Bill out of the chimney.

This scene, while violent in content, hardly inspires sympathy for Bill the lizard, who is depicted as a comic figure prone to physical disasters. Alice's booting him out the chimney reveals her irritability, but the reader doesn't notice her meanness as much as they recognize the humor of a lizard (identified first by Tenniel's illustration, not by Carroll's prose) being propelled from a chimney.

A chorus of voices cries out, "There goes Bill!" as he flies past the roof. Confusion and the rabble of many voices ensue. Bill is found and tended to. The Rabbit, meanwhile, suggests that the house must be burned down. This suggestion reveals the

White Rabbit's tendency to find immediate and extreme remedies without considering all the options. Alice yells out that she will set her cat Dinah on them if they try to set fire to the house. She thinks they should try to take off the roof, but instead she hears the Rabbit ordering a barrowful of something.

The answer to what was ordered is revealed when a shower of pebbles is fired through the window. Some of the pebbles hit Alice. She yells that the pebble throwing better not continue, and silence and a cease fire results. The pebbles in the room turn into little cakes. Believing the cakes will make her smaller, Alice begins swallowing them. Of course, the possibility exists that the cakes could make her larger, but Alice assumes that she can get no larger because there is no more room for her to grow. Denying that possibility and, based upon her past experience, she believes the cakes will cause her to change size. Because she knows she cannot grow larger (although, certainly, the reader knows that it is indeed possible), and doesn't consider that the cakes may have no impact on her size whatsoever, Alice concludes that she should swallow the cakes. Sure enough, she begins to shrink.

After she becomes small enough to fit through the door, Alice runs out of the house and finds a group of animals and birds outside. She notices a Lizard, who turns out to be Bill, being tended to by two guinea pigs. When the other animals come rushing at Alice, she manages to escape by running into the nearby woods.

Alice makes a plan in the woods: She will grow back to her normal size, then she will find the door that opens to the lovely garden. She is considering how to follow through on the plan when she hears a sharp bark overhead. Looking up, she sees a puppy towering over her. He is moving his paw to

Alice ejects Bill the lizard from the White Rabbi's house by booting him through the chimney.
Mary Evans Picture Library

play with her. Alice wants to whistle to him, but she is too frightened by the prospect that the puppy might be hungry. She picks up a stick, and the dog makes a rush for it. Alice manages to avoid being run over, and she runs around with the stick as the puppy jumps about and follows her.

The puppy appears to have come from the real world, an inconsistency in Carroll's text. He exhibits real world characteristics by displaying no anthropomorphic tendencies; the puppy does not speak, wear clothes, or behave in any way unlike a puppy. He does, however, give Alice cause to ponder the puppy's size compared to her own.

When the dog stops a moment to rest, Alice runs away as far as she can—until she runs out of breath and the puppy's barking is far off. While resting, Alice wishes she could have stayed and taught the puppy some tricks, but she realizes the dog is too big for her to play with. The thought of the size of the puppy reminds Alice that she needs to grow again. Looking around, she doesn't see anything that might help her.

A nearby mushroom eventually catches her attention. She approaches it, looks around it, and stands on her tiptoes to peer at the top of the mushroom. A caterpillar is sitting on top, smoking a long hookah. (A hookah is a kind of water pipe associated with the Middle East, with a long flexible tube for drawing smoke through water in a vase or bowl and cooling it. In most instances, a hookah was used for smoking opium or hashish.)

Chapter V: Advice from a Caterpillar

Alice meets a disagreeable Caterpillar smoking a hookah atop a mushroom, gets a valuable tip from the Caterpillar, is mistaken for a serpent by a defensive Pigeon, and comes to a small house.

The Caterpillar and Alice looked at each other for some time in silence: at last the Caterpillar took the hookah out of its mouth, and addressed her in a languid, sleepy voice.

"Who are *you*?" said the Caterpillar.

This was not an encouraging opening for a conversation. Alice replied, rather shyly, "I—I hardly know, sir, just at present—at least I know who I *was* when I got up this morning, but I think I must have been changed several times since then."

"What do you mean by that?" said the Caterpillar sternly. "Explain yourself!"

"I can't explain *myself*, I'm afraid, sir" said Alice, "because I'm not myself, you see."

"I don't see," said the Caterpillar.

"I'm afraid I can't put it more clearly," Alice replied very politely, "for I can't understand it myself to begin with; and being so many different sizes in a day is very confusing."

"It isn't," said the Caterpillar.

"Well, perhaps you haven't found it so yet," said Alice; "but when you have to turn into a chrysalis—you will some day, you know—and then after that into a butterfly, I should think you'll feel it a little queer, won't you?"

"Not a bit," said the Caterpillar.

"Well, perhaps your feelings may be different," said Alice; "all I know is, it would feel very queer to *me*."

"You!" said the Caterpillar contemptuously. "Who are *you*?"

NOTES

Which brought them back again to the beginning of the conversation. Alice felt a little irritated at the Caterpillar's making such *very* short remarks, and she drew herself up and said, very gravely, "I think, you ought to tell me who *you* are, first."

"Why?" said the Caterpillar.

Here was another puzzling question; and as Alice could not think of any good reason, and as the Caterpillar seemed to be in a *very* unpleasant state of mind, she turned away.

"Come back!" the Caterpillar called after her. "I've something important to say!"

This sounded promising, certainly: Alice turned and came back again.

"Keep your temper," said the Caterpillar.

"Is that all?" said Alice, swallowing down her anger as well as she could.

"No," said the Caterpillar.

Alice thought she might as well wait, as she had nothing else to do, and perhaps after all it might tell her something worth hearing. For some minutes it puffed away without speaking, but at last it unfolded its arms, took the hookah out of its mouth again, and said, "So you think you're changed, do you?"

"I'm afraid I am, sir," said Alice; "I can't remember things as I used—and I don't keep the same size for ten minutes together!"

"Can't remember *what* things?" said the Caterpillar.

"Well, I've tried to say '*How doth the little busy bee,*' but it all came different!" Alice replied in a very melancholy voice.

"Repeat, '*You are old, Father William,*'" said the Caterpillar.

Alice folded her hands, and began:

[Handwritten margin notes: "challenging authority. Wouldn't happen in the real world." / "→ ambiguous." / "on top of a mushroom: higher than her." / "caterpillar uses a lot of imperatives: commanding."]

"You are old, Father William," the young man said,
 "And your hair has become very white;
And yet you incessantly stand on your head—
 Do you think, at your age, it is right?"

"In my youth," Father William replied to his son,
 "I feared it might injure the brain;
But, now that I'm perfectly sure I have none,
 Why, I do it again and again."

"You are old," said the youth, "as I mentioned before,
 And have grown most uncommonly fat;
Yet you turned a back-somersault in at the door—
 Pray, what is the reason of that?"

"In my youth," said the **sage**, as he shook his grey locks,
 "I kept all my limbs very supple
By the use of this ointment—one shilling the box—
 Allow me to sell you a couple?"

"You are old," said the youth, "and your jaws are too weak
 For anything tougher than **suet**;
Yet you finished the goose, with the bones and the beak—
 Pray how did you manage to do it?"

"In my youth," said his father, "I took to the law,
 And argued each case with my wife;
And the muscular strength, which it gave to my jaw,
 Has lasted the rest of my life."

"You are old," said the youth, "one would hardly suppose
 That your eye was as steady as ever;
Yet you balanced an eel on the end of your nose—
 What made you so awfully clever?"

"I have answered three questions, and that is enough,"
 Said his father; "don't give yourself **airs**!
Do you think I can listen all day to such stuff?
 Be off, or I'll kick you down stairs!"

sage: a very wise person; especially, an elderly man, widely respected for his wisdom, experience and judgement.

suet: the hard fat deposited around the kidneys and loins of cattle and sheep; used in cooking as a source for tallow (soap).

airs: affected, superior manners and graces.

[handwritten margin notes: role reversal: real poem about age & wisdom. switch of power.]

[handwritten note: → violence.]

"That is not said right," said the Caterpillar.

"Not *quite* right, I'm afraid," said Alice, <u>timidly</u>; "some of the words have got altered."

"It is wrong from beginning to end," said the Caterpillar decidedly, and there was silence for some minutes.

The Caterpillar was the first to speak.

"What size do you want to be?" it asked.

"Oh, I'm not particular as to size," Alice hastily replied; "only one doesn't like changing so often, you know."

"I *don't* know," said the Caterpillar.

Alice said nothing: <u>she had never been so much contradicted in her life before, and she felt that she was losing her temper.</u>

"Are you content now?" said the Caterpillar.

"Well, I should like to be a *little* larger, sir, if you wouldn't mind," said Alice: three inches is such a wretched height to be. *size = power.*

"It is a very good height indeed!" said the Caterpillar angrily, rearing itself upright as it spoke (it was exactly three inches high).

"But I'm not used to it!" pleaded poor Alice in a piteous tone. And she thought of herself, "<u>I wish the creatures wouldn't be so easily offended!</u>"

"You'll get used to it in time," said the Caterpillar; and it put the hookah into its mouth and began smoking again.

This time Alice waited patiently until it chose to speak again. In a minute or two the Caterpillar took the hookah out of its mouth and yawned once or twice, and shook itself. Then it got down off the mushroom, and crawled away in the grass, merely remarking as it went, "One side will make you grow taller, and the other side will make you grow shorter."

"One side of *what*? The other side of *what*?" thought Alice to herself.

Using strategies.

"Of the mushroom," said the Caterpillar, just as slightly creepy. if she had asked it aloud; and in another moment it was out of sight.

Alice remained looking thoughtfully at the mushroom for a minute, trying to make out which were the two sides of it; and as it was perfectly round, she found this a very difficult question. However, at last she stretched her arms round it as far as they would go, and broke off a bit of the edge with each hand.

"And now which is which?" she said to herself, and nibbled a little of the right-hand bit to try the effect: the next moment she felt a violent violence. blow underneath her chin: it had struck her foot! She was a good deal frightened by this very sudden change, but she felt that there was no time to be lost, as she was shrinking rapidly; so she set to work at once to eat some of the other bit. Her chin was pressed so closely against her foot, that there was hardly room to open her mouth; but she did it at last, and managed to swallow a morsel of the left-hand bit.

After eating part of the Caterpillar's mushroom, Alice's body shrinks until her head is resting on her feet.
Mary Evans Picture Library

* * * * * *

"Come, my head's free at last!" said Alice in a tone of delight, which changed into alarm in another moment, when she found that her shoulders were nowhere to be found: all she could see, when she looked down, was an immense length of neck, which seemed to rise like a stalk out of a sea of green leaves that lay far below her.

"What *can* all that green stuff be?" said Alice. "And where *have* my shoulders got to? And oh, my poor hands, how is it I can't see you?" She was moving them about as she spoke, but no result seemed to follow, except a little shaking among the distant green leaves.

As there seemed to be no chance of getting her hands up to her head, she tried to get her head down to them, and was delighted to find that her neck would bend about easily in any direction, like a **serpent**. She had just succeeded in curving it down into a graceful zigzag, and was going to dive in among the leaves, which she found to be nothing but the tops of the trees under which she had been wandering, when a sharp hiss made her draw back in a hurry: a large pigeon had flown into her face, and was beating her violently with its wings.

"Serpent!" screamed the Pigeon.

"I'm *not* a serpent!" said Alice indignantly. "Let me alone!"

"Serpent, I say again!" repeated the Pigeon, but in a more subdued tone, and added with a kind of sob, "I've tried every way, and nothing seems to suit them!"

"I haven't the least idea what you're talking about," said Alice.

"I've tried the roots of trees, and I've tried banks, and I've tried hedges," the Pigeon went on, without attending to her; "but those serpents! There's no pleasing them!"

Alice was more and more puzzled, but she thought there was no use in saying anything more till the Pigeon had finished.

"As if it wasn't trouble enough hatching the eggs," said the Pigeon; "but I must be on the look-out for serpents night and day! Why, I haven't had a wink of sleep these three weeks!"

"I'm very sorry you've been annoyed," said Alice, who was beginning to see its meaning.

"And just as I'd taken the highest tree in the wood," continued the Pigeon, raising its voice to a shriek, "and just as I was thinking I should be free of them at last, they must needs come wriggling down from the sky! Ugh, Serpent!"

serpent: a snake, especially a large, poisonous one.

basing looks on appearances

"But I'm *not* a serpent, I tell you!" said Alice.
"I'm a—I'm a—"

"Well! *What* are you?" said the Pigeon. "I can see you're trying to invent something!"

"I—I'm a little girl," said Alice, rather doubt-fully, as she remembered the number of changes she had gone through that day.

→ identity.

"A likely story indeed!" said the Pigeon in a tone of the deepest contempt. "I've seen a good many little girls in my time, but never *one* with such a neck as that! No, no! You're a serpent; and there's no use denying it. I suppose you'll be telling me next that you never tasted an egg!"

"I *have* tasted eggs, certainly," said Alice, who was a very truthful child; "but little girls eat eggs quite as much as serpents do, you know."

"I don't believe it," said the Pigeon; "but if they do, why then they're a kind of serpent, that's all I can say."

This was such a new idea to Alice, that she was quite silent for a minute or two, which gave the Pigeon the opportunity of adding, "You're look-ing for eggs, I know *that* well enough; and what does it matter to me whether you're a little girl or a serpent?"

"It matters a good deal to *me*," said Alice hastily; "but I'm not looking for eggs, as it happens; and if I was, I shouldn't want *yours*: I don't like them raw."

"Well, be off, then!" said the Pigeon in a sulky tone, as it settled down again into its nest. Alice crouched down among the trees as well as she could, for her neck kept getting entangled among the branches, and every now and then she had to stop and untwist it. After a while she remembered that she still held the pieces of mushroom in her hands, and she set to work very carefully, nibbling first at one and then at the other, and growing sometimes taller and sometimes shorter, until she had succeeded in bringing herself down to her usual height. It was so long since she had been anything near the right size, that it felt quite strange at first; but she got used to it in a few minutes, and began talking to herself, as usual. "Come, there's half my plan done now! How puzzling all these changes are! I'm never sure what I'm going to be, from one minute to another! However, I've got back to my right size: the next thing is, to get into that beautiful garden—how *is* that to be done, I wonder?" As she said this, she came suddenly upon an open place, with a little house in it about four feet high. "Whoever lives there," thought Alice, "it'll never do to come upon them *this* size: why, I should frighten them out of their wits!" So she began nibbling at the right-hand bit again, and did not venture to go near the house till she had brought herself down to nine-inches high.

[handwritten annotation: → adjusting maturing.]

COMMENTARY

In this chapter, Carroll playfully discusses the nature of personal identity. After the Caterpillar and Alice look at each other for a while, the Caterpillar removes the hookah (smoking pipe) from his mouth and asks, "Who are *you?*" Alice fumbles for an answer because of all the different changes she has gone through that day. The Caterpillar requests an explanation, but Alice has none. She tells him, "I'm not myself, you see."

Each time Alice tries to explain her confusion, the Caterpillar replies with a negative statement: To Alice's assertion that she is not herself, "you see," the Caterpillar replies, "I don't see." Alice has used a figure of speech known as synesthesia, in which the qualities of two or more human senses are blended. For example, an individual may say that he or she hears colors or feels that someone has touched his or her heart; but a literal interpretation would result simply in confusion.

When Alice asks the Caterpillar if he sees, he replies that he does not; he cannot tell from viewing Alice that she is any different from how she was in the past. The Caterpillar has no empirical knowledge of who or what Alice had been prior to his meeting her for the first time. What Alice means to say is "do you understand?" to which the Caterpillar's response is appropriate, "Explain yourself!"

Alice continues, saying that undergoing so many changes in size is confusing, to which the Caterpillar responds, "It isn't." Alice suggests that when the Caterpillar turns into a butterfly, the transition will feel a little queer, to which the Caterpillar replies, "Not a bit." Alice says that "it would feel very queer to *me*," and the Caterpillar returns to his original question: "Who are *you*?" The Caterpillar cannot "see" nor "understand" Alice's predicament because her situation is so alien to his experience of reality. He accepts as a matter of course that he will evolve from a caterpillar to a chrysalis to a moth or butterfly. Because Alice's changes into maturity will be more gradual, she cannot comprehend the nature of such sudden and drastic change, even though her most recent experiences could have easily prepared her to accept the Caterpillar's fate.

Alice tries to turn the line of questioning around and have the Caterpillar identify himself, but her tactic of shifting attention from herself fails. The Caterpillar challenges her

question as to his identity with the question, "Why?" With such puzzling questions confronting her, as well as the Caterpillar's unpleasant tone, Alice decides to leave. The Caterpillar asks her to come

Alice peers over the mushroom cap as she speaks to the Caterpillar.
Mary Evans Picture Library

back, saying he has something important to tell her. When Alice returns, he tells her to keep her temper. Alice wonders if this is all the Caterpillar has to offer.

The Caterpillar puffs on his hookah for a while. Finally, he asks her, "So you think you're changed, do you?" Alice replies that she can't remember things and can't seem to stay the same size. The Caterpillar requests that she recite the poem "You are old, Father William." By this request, the Caterpillar seems to suggest that if Alice can remember a verse then she will have discerned a continuum of memories that will help her define her identity. Because Alice seems convinced that she once knew the poem, she can prove her sanity by reciting it again. Her recitation is wrong from beginning to end, however, and the end result is a perfect segue into a parody of Robert Southey's "The Old Man's Comforts and How He Gained Them."

The poem itself is a silly nonsense poem about a young man questioning Father William about his exploits. William "incessantly stand[s] on his head," which, he says, will not hurt his brain because he has none. He has grown rotund in his old age, but remains limber enough to turn somersaults, the result, he tells the young man, of an ointment he is willing to sell the young man. The young man brings to William's attention that William's jaws are incredibly strong. William explains that because he practiced law against his wife he has exercised his jaw enough for the "rest of my life." As he balances an eel on the end of his nose, William tells the young man that he'll not answer any more questions.

After Alice completes the verse, the Caterpillar informs her that she did not recite the verse correctly. Alice agrees that she got some of the words wrong, but the Caterpillar maintains that she got the verse wrong from beginning to end. As this is the second instance of Alice reciting a verse incorrectly, it perhaps indicates Alice's inability to adapt her language to convey what she is thinking. It also could represent that Alice is dreaming and cannot stop herself from incorrectly reciting the verses—a common occurrence in dreaming where the dreamer imagines him or herself performing an otherwise simple task improperly.

After another long silence, the Caterpillar inquires as to what size Alice wants to be. Alice states that size doesn't matter, she just "doesn't like changing so often, you know." This remark can be construed as rude, particularly in the presence of a caterpillar.

Again, the Caterpillar replies defensively that he doesn't "know." Alice's statement infers a common ground that she and the Caterpillar do not share. He cannot know because it is his nature to change drastically at several points in his life. Alice begins to feel angry about being contradicted so often. Responding to a query by the Caterpillar about whether she is content with her current size, Alice says that she wants to be taller, because "three inches is such a wretched height to be." The Caterpillar again contradicts her because he himself is quite content with his own height of exactly three inches.

Alice asserts that she wishes the creatures weren't so easily offended. The Caterpillar tells her that she will get used to it. The Caterpillar returns to his hookah. After awhile he yawns, gets up, and crawls away. His parting words to Alice are, "One side will make you grow taller, and the other side will make you grow shorter." As she wonders what "sides" the Caterpillar is speaking of, he adds, "of the mushroom."

Whether Carroll knew the hallucinogenic properties of certain mushrooms has never been proven or disproved. Appearing so close in the story to the hookah-smoking Caterpillar, however, indicates that he might have heard or read something about "magic mushrooms." On the other hand, Carroll may have simply been using a device common in many fairy stories—the mushroom or toadstool that houses the residents of fairyland.

Because the mushroom top is round, determining which side is left and which is right is a difficult task for Alice. Again, Carroll seems to point out language's inability to reliably convey necessary information in a clear and concise way. Alice spreads her arms along both sides and breaks off portions with her hands. She nibbles at a portion in her right hand: Suddenly, her chin strikes her foot. She becomes so small that she can barely open her mouth, but she manages to bite some mushroom from her left hand.

Alice's head rises up from her shoes, which makes her happy, but that soon changes: Her neck grows so long that when she looks down she cannot even see her shoulders. Her neck and head rise above the tops of the trees. She cannot see her hands, so she has no chance to take a quick nibble from the piece of mushroom in her right hand to reduce her size. However, she is able to bend her neck easily to swoop and curve around. She twists among the tops of trees, like a serpent.

"Serpent!," in fact, is screamed at her by a Pigeon that is flapping her wings against Alice's face. Alice protests that she is not a serpent. The Pigeon complains that she has tried to hide her eggs in the roots of trees, riverbanks, and hedges, but serpents persist in finding "them." Alice is unclear as to what "them" infers. Alice is puzzled until the Pigeon explains that hatching eggs is difficult enough, but she also has to be wary of serpents and hasn't been able to sleep for three weeks. Alice begins to sympathize. The Pigeon explains that she thinks she is safe when she moves her nest to the top of a tree, until Alice came "wriggling down from the sky! Ugh, Serpent!"

Alice contends that she is not a serpent, but her hesitancy when identifying herself as a little girl leads the Pigeon to conclude that the claim is "A likely story indeed!" The Pigeon asserts that she has seen a good many little girls in her time, and Alice bore much more of a resemblance to a serpent. She challenges Alice by asking her whether or not she has eaten eggs. Alice replies that she has, and points out that little girls eat eggs as much as serpents do. If so, counters the Pigeon, then little girls are a kind of serpent—a reply that Alice considers. This seemingly correct, yet actually incorrect, method of reasoning (known as a syllogism) enables the Pigeon to thwart logic to prove her point, thus further confusing Alice's identity crisis.

While Alice thinks about the remark, the Pigeon adds that Alice is looking for eggs. Therefore, whether Alice is a serpent or a little girl doesn't matter to the Pigeon. "It matters a good deal to *me*," Alice counters, then she adds that she isn't looking for eggs and she wouldn't eat raw eggs, anyway. If Alice wasn't looking for eggs then, the Pigeon concludes, she should go away, and the Pigeon sits down in her nest.

While maneuvering among the trees, Alice has to stop occasionally to untangle herself when her neck becomes twisted in the branches. She is eventually able to wind her head down to her hands and nibble some of the mushroom, taking a bit from each hand until she is able to return to her normal height. How can Alice remember what her normal height is, however, relative to the surroundings in which she finds herself? Because she has changed sizes so much to accommodate where she happens to find herself, she cannot reasonably determine what her correct size is. Finding a size with which she is comfortable takes her a while, but soon she begins walking and, as usual, talking to herself. She devises a plan to get to the lovely garden she spied through the small door. While walking and wondering about the puzzling changes she has undergone, Alice arrives at a house about four-feet high.

She nibbles at the mushroom in her right hand to reduce her size so as not to frighten the occupants of the house. When she is reduced to nine-inches tall, she is ready to venture into the house.

Chapter VI: Pig and Pepper

In a noisy kitchen filled with the smell of smoke and pepper, Alice meets the Duchess, is given the care of a baby that turns into a pig, and makes friends with the grinning Cheshire Cat.

For a minute or two she stood looking at the house, and wondering what to do next, when suddenly a **footman in livery** came running out of the wood—(she considered him to be a footman because he was in livery: otherwise, judging by his face only, she would have called him a fish)— and rapped loudly at the door with his knuckles. It was opened by another footman in livery, with a round face, and large eyes like a frog; and both footmen, Alice noticed, had powdered hair that curled all over their heads. She felt very curious to know what it was all about, and crept a little way out of the wood to listen.

The Fish-Footman began by producing from under his arm a great letter, nearly as large as himself, and this he handed over to the other, saying, in a solemn tone, "For the Duchess. An invitation from the Queen to play croquet." The Frog-Footman repeated, in the same solemn tone, only changing the order of the words a little, "From the Queen. An invitation for the Duchess to play croquet."

Then they both bowed low, and their curls got entangled together.

Alice laughed so much at this, that she had to run back into the wood for fear of their hearing her; and when she next peeped out the Fish-Footman was gone, and the other was sitting on the ground near the door, staring stupidly up into the sky.

Alice went timidly up to the door, and knocked. "There's no sort of use in knocking," said the Footman, "and that for two reasons. First,

NOTES

footman: a male servant who assists the butler in a large household.

in livery: an identifying uniform worn by servants.

appearances.

servitude.

size.

word order is reversed & confused.

she starts off polite but then grows more confident.

because I'm on the same side of the door as you
are; secondly, because they're making such a
noise inside, no one could possibly hear you."
And certainly there was a most extraordinary
noise going on within—a constant howling and
sneezing, and every now and then a great crash,
as if a dish or kettle had been broken to pieces.
"Please, then," said Alice, "how am I to get in?"
"There might be some sense in your knocking,"
the Footman went on without attending to her,   *language change.*
"if we had the door between us. For instance, if
you were *inside*, you might knock, and I could
let you out, you know." He was looking up into
the sky all the time he was speaking, and this   *footman: pompous*
Alice thought decidedly uncivil. "But perhaps he   *distracted.*
can't help it," she said to herself; "his eyes are so
very nearly at the top of his head. But at any rate
he might answer questions.—How am I to get
in?" she repeated, aloud.
"I shall sit here," the Footman remarked, "till
tomorrow—"
At this moment the door of the house opened,
and a large plate came skimming out, straight
at the Footman's head: it just grazed his nose,   *Violence.*
and broke to pieces against one of the trees
behind him.
"—or next day, maybe," the Footman continued   *Footman is used to the*
in the same tone, exactly as if nothing had   *violent.*
happened.
"How am I to get in?" asked Alice again, in a
louder tone. *getting less timid.*
"*Are* you to get in at all?" said the Footman.
"That's the first question, you know."
It was, no doubt: only Alice did not like to be
told so. "It's really dreadful," she muttered to
herself, "the way all the creatures argue. It's
enough to drive one crazy!"
                    but are they already are?

The Footman seemed to think this a good opportunity for repeating his remark, with variations. "I shall sit here," he said, "on and off, for days and days."

"But what am I to do?" said Alice.

"Anything you like," said the Footman, and began whistling.

"Oh, there's no use in talking to him," said Alice desperately: "he's perfectly idiotic!" And she opened the door and went in.

The door led right into a large kitchen, which was full of smoke from one end to the other: the Duchess was sitting on a three-legged stool in the middle, nursing a baby; the cook was leaning over the fire, stirring a large **cauldron** which seemed to be full of soup.

"There's certainly too much pepper in that soup!" Alice said to herself, as well as she could for sneezing.

There was certainly too much of it in the air. Even the Duchess sneezed occasionally; and as for the baby, it was sneezing and howling alternately without a moment's pause. The only things in the kitchen that did not sneeze, were the cook, and a large cat which was sitting on the hearth and grinning from ear to ear.

"Please would you tell me," said Alice, a little timidly, for she was not quite sure whether it was good manners for her to speak first, "why your cat grins like that?"

"It's a **Cheshire cat**," said the Duchess, "and that's why. Pig!"

She said the last word with such sudden violence that Alice quite jumped; but she saw in another moment that it was addressed to the baby, and not to her, so she took courage, and went on again:—

bathos

juxtaposition.

Duchess, go round looking pretty.

cauldron (also spelled "caldron"): a large kettle for boiling.

authority figures.

Cheshire cat: a cat from Cheshire, a county in West England.

cheshire cheese, shaped like a cat.

building up expectation.

"I didn't know that Cheshire cats always grinned; in fact, I didn't know that cats *could* grin."

"They all can," said the Duchess; "and most of 'em do." *unsuited to classic Duchess.*

"I don't know of any that do," Alice said very politely, feeling quite pleased to have got into a conversation.

"You don't know much," said the Duchess; "and that's a fact." *rude.* Hunt. → *a characteristic Alice shares.*

just her title makes Alice respect her.

Alice did not at all like the tone of this remark, and thought it would be as well to introduce some other subject of conversation. While she was trying to fix on one, the cook took the cauldron of soup off the fire, and at once set to work throwing everything within her reach at the - Duchess and the baby—the fire-irons came first; then followed a shower of saucepans, plates, and dishes. The Duchess took no notice of them even when they hit her; and the baby was howling so much already, that it was quite impossible to say whether the blows hurt it or not.

VIOLENCE.

"Oh, *please* mind what you're doing!" cried Alice, jumping up and down in an agony of terror.

"Oh, there goes his *precious* nose"; as an unusually large saucepan flew close by it, and very nearly carried it off.

"If everybody minded their own business," the Duchess said in a hoarse growl, "the world would go round a deal faster than it does."

"Which would *not* be an advantage," said Alice, who felt very glad to get an opportunity of showing off a little of her knowledge. "Just think of what work it would make with the day and night! You see the earth takes twenty-four hours to turn round on its axis—"

"Talking of axes," said the Duchess, "chop off her head!"

homophone: play on words.

Alice glanced rather anxiously at the cook, to see
if she meant to take the hint; but the cook was
busily stirring the soup, and seemed not to be listening, so she went on again: "Twenty-four
hours, I *think*; or is it twelve? I—"
"Oh, don't bother *me*," said the Duchess; "I
never could abide figures!" And with that she
began nursing her child again, singing a sort of
lullaby to it as she did so, and giving it a violent
shake at the end of every line:

> *"Speak roughly to your little boy,*
> *And beat him when he sneezes:*
> *He only does it to annoy,*
> *Because he knows it teases."*

uneducated.

Bad mother by our standards. but not Victorian.

CHORUS
(In which the cook and the baby joined):
"Wow! wow! wow!"

PARODY

While the Duchess sang the second verse of the
song, she kept tossing the baby violently up and
down, and the poor little thing howled so, that
Alice could hardly hear the words:

> *"I speak severely to my boy,*
> *I beat him when he sneezes;*
> *For he can thoroughly enjoy*
> *The pepper when he pleases!"*

CHORUS
"Wow! wow! wow!"

"Here! you may nurse it a bit, if you like!" the
Duchess said to Alice, flinging the baby at her as
she spoke. "I must go and get ready to play
croquet with the Queen," and she hurried out of

*croquet: an outdoor game in which the players use mal-
lets to drive a wooden ball through a series of hoops
placed in the ground.*

the room. The cook threw a frying-pan after her
as she went out, but it just missed her.

Alice caught the baby with some difficulty, as it
was a queer-shaped little creature, and held out
its arms and legs in all directions, "just like a
star-fish," thought Alice. The poor little thing
was snorting like a steam-engine when she
caught it, and kept doubling itself up and
straightening itself out again, so that altogether,
for the first minute or two, it was as much as she
could do to hold it.

As soon as she had made out the proper way of
nursing it (which was to twist it up into a sort of
knot, and then keep tight hold of its right ear
and left foot, so as to prevent its undoing itself),
she carried it out into the open air. "*If* I don't
take this child away with me," thought Alice,
"they're sure to kill it in a day or two: wouldn't it
be murder to leave it behind?" She said the last
words out loud, and the little thing grunted in
reply (it had left off sneezing by this time).
'Don't grunt,' said Alice; "that's not at all a
proper way of expressing yourself."
The baby grunted again, and Alice looked very
anxiously into its face to see what was the matter
with it. There could be no doubt that it had a
very turn-up nose, much more like a snout than
a real nose; also its eyes were getting extremely
small for a baby: altogether Alice did not like the
look of the thing at all. "But perhaps it was only
sobbing," she thought, and looked into its eyes
again, to see if there were any tears.

No, there were no tears. "If you're going to turn
into a pig, my dear," said Alice, seriously, "I'll
have nothing more to do with you. Mind now!"
The poor little thing sobbed again (or grunted, it
was impossible to say which), and they went on
for some while in silence.

Alice was just beginning to think to herself, "Now, what am I to do with this creature when I get it home?" when it grunted again, so violently, that she looked down into its face in some alarm. This time there could be *no* mistake about it: it was neither more nor less than a pig, and she felt that it would be quite absurd for her to carry it further.

So she set the little creature down, and felt quite relieved to see it trot away quietly into the wood. "If it had grown up," she said to herself, "it would have made a dreadfully ugly child: but it makes rather a handsome pig, I think." And she began thinking over other children she knew, who might do very well as pigs, and was just saying to herself, "if one only knew the right way to change them—" when she was a little startled by seeing the Cheshire Cat sitting on a bough of a tree a few yards off.

The Cat only grinned when it saw Alice. It looked good-natured, she thought: still it had *very* long claws and a great many teeth, so she felt that it ought to be treated with respect.

"Cheshire Puss," she began, rather timidly, as she did not at all know whether it would like the name: however, it only grinned a little wider. "Come, it's pleased so far," thought Alice, and she went on. "Would you tell me, please, which way I ought to go from here?"

"That depends a good deal on where you want to get to," said the Cat.

"I don't much care where—" said Alice.

"Then it doesn't matter which way you go," said the Cat.

"—so long as I get *somewhere*," Alice added as an explanation.

"Oh, you're sure to do that," said the Cat, "if you only walk long enough."

Alice spots the Cheshire Cat smiling down at her from the branch of a tree.
Mary Evans Picture Library

comparing with others.

appearances.

cheshire cat: real world logic.

logical: it's true. not much use though.

Alice felt that this could not be denied, so she tried another question. "What sort of people live about here?"

"In *that* direction," the Cat said, waving its right paw round, "lives a Hatter: and in *that* direction," waving the other paw, "lives a March Hare. Visit either you like: they're both mad."

"But I don't want to go among mad people," Alice remarked.

"Oh, you can't help that," said the Cat: "we're all mad here. I'm mad. You're mad."

"How do you know I'm mad?" said Alice.

"You must be," said the Cat, "or you wouldn't have come here."

Alice didn't think that proved it at all; however, she went on "And how do you know that you're mad?"

"To begin with," said the Cat, "a dog's not mad. You grant that?"

"I suppose so," said Alice.

"Well, then," the Cat went on, "you see, a dog growls when it's angry, and wags its tail when it's pleased. Now I growl when I'm pleased, and wag my tail when I'm angry. Therefore I'm mad."

"I call it purring, not growling," said Alice.

"Call it what you like," said the Cat. "Do you play croquet with the Queen to-day?"

"I should like it very much," said Alice, "but I haven't been invited yet."

"You'll see me there," said the Cat, and vanished. Alice was not much surprised at this, she was getting so used to queer things happening. While she was looking at the place where it had been, it suddenly appeared again.

"By-the-bye, what became of the baby?" said the Cat. "I'd nearly forgotten to ask."

"It turned into a pig," Alice quietly said, just as if it had come back in a natural way.

"I thought it would," said the Cat, and vanished again.

Alice waited a little, half expecting to see it again, but it did not appear, and after a minute or two she walked on in the direction in which the March Hare was said to live. "I've seen hatters before," she said to herself; "the March Hare will be much the most interesting, and perhaps as this is May it won't be raving mad—at least not so mad as it was in March." As she said this, she looked up, and there was the Cat again, sitting on a branch of a tree.

double t.

irrelevant.

"Did you say pig, or fig?" said the Cat.

"I said pig," replied Alice; "and I wish you wouldn't keep appearing and vanishing so suddenly: you make one quite giddy."

→ more confident.

"All right," said the Cat; and this time it vanished quite slowly, beginning with the end of the tail, and ending with the grin, which remained some time after the rest of it had gone.

language: reversed.

"Well! I've often seen a cat without a grin," thought Alice; "but a grin without a cat! It's the most curious thing I ever saw in my life!"

→ is it?

She had not gone much farther before she came in sight of the house of the March Hare: she thought it must be the right house, because the chimneys were shaped like ears and the roof was thatched with fur. It was so large a house, that she did not like to go nearer till she had nibbled some more of the left-hand bit of mushroom, and raised herself to about two feet high: even then she walked up towards it rather timidly, saying to herself, "Suppose it should be raving mad after all! I almost wish I'd gone to see the Hatter instead!"

→ appearances

size = power.

scared of madness

COMMENTARY

In this chapter, Carroll introduces characters that will appear in subsequent chapters. Although the White Rabbit appears throughout the story and Bill the Lizard appears at the trial in Chapters XI and XII, no other characters introduced in the first five chapters appear afterwards.

Much of this chapter is notable for the violence displayed by both the Duchess and the cook, as well as the strange and often disturbing characteristics of the Cheshire Cat, who can disappear wholly or partially at will. The figure of a cat's head hovering above Alice is one of the book's most enduring images.

After shrinking to nine-inches tall, Alice approaches the four-foot-tall house. Standing near the house, she identifies a footman who is running from the woods and knocks on the door of the house. Another footman opens the door. Both the footman who knocked (a fish) and the one who answered (a frog) are wearing powdered wigs. Alice retreats out of sight to listen to their conversation.

The Fish-Footman produces a letter that is nearly as long as he is. He hands the letter to the Frog-Footman and announces with great solemnity an invitation to the Duchess from the Queen to play croquet. When the footmen bow to each other, their wigs became entangled. Alice laughs so hard at the spectacle that she runs and hides behind a tree so she won't be heard. (Carroll may be lampooning the pomp and circumstance of the landed gentry by displaying the two footmen wearing outdated and impractical regalia.) When Alice looks back at the house, the Fish-Footman is gone and the Frog-Footman is sitting on the ground looking at the sky.

Alice walks slowly up to the door and knocks. The Footman informs her that there is no use in

The Fish-Footman presents a letter to the Frog-Footman. It is an invitation to the Duchess from the Queen to play croquet.
Mary Evans Picture Library

knocking, for he is on the same side of the door as she is and the noise within is too great for her knock to be heard. There is a great commotion inside—howling, sneezing, and occasional crashes of dishes being smashed into pieces. The Footman ponders aloud the question of whether knocking would be useful, looking at the sky the entire time rather than looking directly at the person (Alice) he is addressing as English social manners normally dictate. His inability to look at Alice offends her. By this, Carroll seems to make fun of foolishly adhering to specific elements of Victorian societal decorum when Alice thinks it rude that the Footman speaks while looking at the sky and not at her. She then realizes that frogs have eyes nearly at the top of their head and the Footman cannot help but look upward.

The door to the house opens, and a plate comes sailing out. It grazes the Footman's nose and crashes against a tree. The Footman considers how long he will sit in place. Alice asks him how to get into the house, but the Footman reverses the question to, "*Are* you to get in at all?" Alice mutters to herself that the way creatures continue to argue with her is dreadful. Meanwhile, the Footman returns to his musings about how long he will sit in place. Exasperated, Alice pronounces the Footman a fool and opens the door on her own. Victorians would have interpreted Alice's actions as presumptuously rude.

Alice enters through the door and immediately finds herself in a kitchen. A Duchess is sitting on a three-legged stool in the middle of the kitchen, holding a howling baby. A cook stands by a stove stirring a cauldron. Smoke and the smell of pepper fill the air. The pepper is so prominent that Alice, the Duchess, and the howling baby sneeze frequently. The cook and a grinning cat are the only ones not sneezing.

Alice asks the Duchess why the cat is grinning. "It's a Cheshire Cat," says the Duchess, "and that's why. Pig!" The last remark, Alice discovers, is intended for the baby. The reply—the cat grins because it is a Cheshire Cat—reflects the kind of simple logic used by many characters in Wonderland. The phrase "grins like a Cheshire Cat" may have derived from inns in Cheshire, England, that had signs with smiling lions on them.

Alice states that she did not know cats could grin. "They all can," replies the Duchess, to which Alice contends that she doesn't know any that grin. "You don't know much," says the Duchess, a remark that displeases Alice. She begins to think of a different subject to discuss when the cook

puts down her spoon and begins throwing objects at the Duchess. She tosses fire irons, saucepans, plates, and dishes, some of which hit the Duchess or her howling baby. This violence is, by today's standards, shocking and horrible. Putting a baby in danger may be the darkest of dark humor.

Alice asks the cook to stop, but the Duchess remarks that the world would go around faster if everyone minded their own business. Such pronouncements become a regular bill of fare with the Duchess. She will later display her habit of making hasty assumptions that she passes off as fact to whomever will listen. For example, when the

Alice jumps up and down and demands that the cook stop throwing plates and fire irons before the baby is hurt.
Mary Evans Picture Library

Duchess attends the croquet game in Chapter IX, she embarks on a series of such "morals" as "flamingoes and mustard both bite. And the moral of that is—'Birds of a feather flock together.'" Making the world go around faster would not be an advantage, replies Alice. She explains that a faster-moving world would upset the balance of day and night and makes the incorrect supposition that a shorter day would mean that individuals would need to work harder. She points out that the earth takes twenty-four hours to turn on its axis. "Talking of axes," said the Duchess, "chop off her head!"

Alice looks anxiously at the cook, who is busy stirring the cauldron. Alice continues quoting figures about the hours in a day, but the Duchess grows impatient and begins singing a lullaby to the baby. The lullaby has violent words, and the Duchess shakes the baby at the end of each line. After she ends the lullaby, the Duchess tosses the baby to Alice and announces that she is off to play croquet with the Queen. The cook flings a frying pan at the Duchess as she leaves, just missing her.

Alice determines that it would be murder to leave the baby in the house with all of its violence, and considers kidnapping him. Her assessment is incorrect, however, because neglecting to rescue the baby is not equal to murder. She is also incorrect in assuming the baby is a child. After she is outside, however, the child stops sneezing and howling, but begins grunting. Alice looks at the child for the first time: It has a snout, rather than a nose, and its eyes are very small. She wonders what she should do with the child. When it grunts again, Alice looks at it: No doubt, it has turned into a pig. She puts it on the ground, and the pig runs away into the woods.

Alice thinks about pigs and children. The creature she held made an ugly child, she considers, but makes an attractive pig. In this, Carroll seems to draw attention to the relative merits humans

Alice is surprised to find that the child she saved from the cook's rage has turned into a grunting pig.
Mary Evans Picture Library

ascribe to beauty. Traits attractive in an animal are unattractive when shared by a human and vice versa. Alice notices the Cheshire Cat sitting in a nearby tree. The grinning Cat has many teeth and long claws, Alice notes, and needs to be treated with respect. She addresses him as "Cheshire Puss," and asks him for advice on where to go next.

"That depends a good deal on where you want to get to," says the Cat. Alice replies that she doesn't really care where she goes, to which the Cat asserts that it doesn't matter, then, which way she walks. The Cat cannot give her a specific destination if her question is vague from the beginning. With the line of questioning leading nowhere, Alice inquires about the sort of people who live around there.

The Cat motions with his right paw to the direction where a Hatter lives, and with his left paw to the direction where a March Hare lives. "They're both mad," the Cat informs Alice. She replies that she doesn't want to be among mad people, to which the Cat responds, "we're all mad." When Alice asks why the Cat thinks she is mad, the Cat reasons that she must be, otherwise she wouldn't be there.

Alice doesn't agree that the Cat's assertion proves she is mad. Changing her tactic, Alice asks the Cat why he believes that he is mad. The Cat replies with faulty logic, beginning with the premise that a dog is not mad, to which Alice agrees. A dog growls when it is angry and wags its tail when it is happy. But, the Cat asserts that he growls when he is pleased and wags his tail when he's angry, which he believes proves that he is insane. And when measured against the criteria applied to judging the sanity of a dog, the Cat is correct. The Cat, however, is not a dog, so the rules for judging its sanity do not apply. Because a dog does many things opposite of what a cat does, the Cat concludes his line of reasoning by asserting that cats who don't behave like dogs (considered sane by Alice) are mad. But the end result is the same as if the Cat had told her that he was lying and was always a liar. The statement then calls into question whether it is a double negative, which makes a positive.

The Cat asks Alice if she plans to play croquet with the Queen, adding that Alice will see the Cat there, and then he vanishes. Alice continues looking at the place where the Cheshire Cat had been, and he reappears. The Cat inquires about the baby. Alice answers that the baby had turned into a pig. "I thought it would," says the Cat, and he vanishes again. Because the Cat has revealed previously that he is insane, such a revelation as a baby turning into a pig likely would not be a surprising occurrence.

After waiting for the Cat to reappear, which he doesn't, Alice decides to go see the March Hare. She reasons that she has seen Hatters before. Furthermore, because it was May, the Hare was not likely to be as mad as he was in March.

Looking up in the tree again, Alice watches the Cat reappear. The Cat asks whether she had said the child turned into a "pig" or a "fig." Alice responds that she had said "pig," and informs the Cat that his sudden vanishing and reappearing makes her giddy. The Cat then fades very slowly, beginning with his tail and ending with only the grin remaining. The cat's disappearance and partial reappearance has caused critics to speculate about the Cheshire Cat being inspired by Cheshire cheeses of Carroll's time. Such cheeses were carved in the shape of a grinning cat. When eaten from one end to the other, the cat would be left with only its head and, eventually, its mouth. "I've often seen a cat without a grin," notes Alice, but a grin without a cat is "the most curious thing I ever saw in my life!"

She walks off and soon reaches the March Hare's house. She identifies it as such because it has chimneys shaped like rabbit ears and a roof thatched with soft fur. It is a large house, so Alice nibbles some mushroom from her left hand to grow to two feet in height. She moves timidly toward the house, and wonders whether she should have visited the Hatter instead.

Chapter VII: A Mad Tea-Party

Alice takes tea with a Hatter, the March Hare, and a Dormouse, engages in confusing wordplay, and nearly hears the Dormouse's tale of three sisters who lived in a well.

There was a table set out under a tree in front of the house, and the **March Hare** and the **Hatter** were having tea at it: a **Dormouse** was sitting between them, fast asleep, and the other two were using it as a cushion, resting their elbows on it, and talking over its head. "Very uncomfortable for the Dormouse," thought Alice; "only, as it's asleep, I suppose it doesn't mind." The table was a large one, but the three were all crowded together at one corner of it: "No room! No room!" they cried out when they saw Alice coming. "There's *plenty* of room!" said Alice indignantly, and she sat down in a large arm-chair at one end of the table.

"Have some wine," the March Hare said in an encouraging tone.

Alice looked all round the table, but there was nothing on it but tea. "I don't see any wine," she remarked.

"There isn't any," said the March Hare.

"Then it wasn't very civil of you to offer it," said Alice angrily.

"It wasn't very civil of you to sit down without being invited," said the March Hare.

"I didn't know it was *your* table," said Alice; "it's laid for a great many more than three."

"Your hair wants cutting," said the Hatter. He had been looking at Alice for some time with great curiosity, and this was his first speech.

"You should learn not to make personal remarks," Alice said with some severity; "it's very rude."

NOTES

March Hare: a hare in breeding time, proverbially regarded as an example of madness.

hatter: a person who makes, sells, or cleans hats, especially men's hats.

dormouse: any of a family of small, furry-tailed, mostly tree-dwelling Old World rodents.

→ assertive.

The Hatter opened his eyes very wide on hearing this; but all he *said* was, "Why is a raven like a writing-desk?"

"Come, we shall have some fun now!" thought Alice. "I'm glad they've begun asking riddles.— I believe I can guess that," she added aloud.

"Do you mean that you think you can find out the answer to it?" said the March Hare.

"Exactly so," said Alice.

"Then you should say what you mean," the March Hare went on.

"I do," Alice hastily replied; "at least—at least I mean what I say—that's the same thing, you know."

"Not the same thing a bit!" said the Hatter. "You might just as well say that 'I see what I eat' is the same thing as 'I eat what I see'!"

"You might just as well say," added the March Hare, "that 'I like what I get' is the same thing as 'I get what I like'!"

"You might just as well say," added the Dormouse, who seemed to be talking in his sleep, "that 'I breathe when I sleep' is the same thing as 'I sleep when I breathe'!"

"It *is* the same thing with you," said the Hatter, and here the conversation dropped, and the party sat silent for a minute, while Alice thought over all she could remember about ravens and writing-desks, which wasn't much.

The Hatter was the first to break the silence. "What day of the month is it?" he said, turning to Alice: he had taken his watch out of his pocket, and was looking at it uneasily, shaking it every now and then, and holding it to his ear.

Alice considered a little, and then said "The fourth."

"Two days wrong!" sighed the Hatter. "I told you **butter wouldn't suit the works**!" he added looking angrily at the March Hare.

Wordplay

epistemology: limits of language

"butter wouldn't suit the works:" the March Hare has tried to lubricate the watch's gears using butter.

"It was the *best* butter," the March Hare meekly replied.

"Yes, but some crumbs must have got in as well," the Hatter grumbled: "you shouldn't have put it in with the bread-knife."

The March Hare took the watch and looked at it gloomily: then he dipped it into his cup of tea, and looked at it again: but he could think of nothing better to say than his first remark, "It was the *best* butter, you know."

Alice had been looking over his shoulder with some curiosity. "What a funny watch!" she remarked. "It tells the day of the month, and doesn't tell what o'clock it is!"

"Why should it?" muttered the Hatter. "Does *your* watch tell you what year it is?"

"Of course not," Alice replied very readily: "but that's because it stays the same year for such a long time together."

"Which is just the case with *mine*," said the Hatter. Alice felt dreadfully puzzled. The Hatter's remark seemed to have no sort of meaning in it, and yet it was certainly English. "I don't quite understand you," she said, as politely as she could.

"The Dormouse is asleep again," said the Hatter, and he poured a little hot tea upon its nose.

The Dormouse shook its head impatiently, and said, without opening its eyes, "Of course, of course; just what I was going to remark myself."

"Have you guessed the riddle yet?" the Hatter said, turning to Alice again.

"No, I give it up," Alice replied: "what's the answer?"

"I haven't the slightest idea," said the Hatter.

"Nor I," said the March Hare.

Alice sighed wearily. "I think you might do something better with the time," she said, "than waste it in asking riddles that have no answers."

"If you knew Time as well as I do," said the Hatter, "you wouldn't talk about wasting *it*. It's *him*."

"I don't know what you mean," said Alice.

"Of course you don't!" the Hatter said, tossing his head contemptuously. "I dare say you never even spoke to Time!"

"Perhaps not," Alice cautiously replied: "but I know I have to beat time when I learn music."

"Ah! that accounts for it," said the Hatter. "He won't stand beating. Now, if you only kept on good terms with him, he'd do almost anything you liked with the clock. For instance, suppose it were nine o'clock in the morning, just time to begin lessons: you'd only have to whisper a hint to Time, and round goes the clock in a twinkling! Half-past one, time for dinner!"

("I only wish it was," the March Hare said to itself in a whisper.)

"That would be grand, certainly," said Alice thoughtfully: "but then—I shouldn't be hungry for it, you know."

"Not at first, perhaps," said the Hatter: "but you could keep it to half-past one as long as you liked."

"Is that the way you manage?" Alice asked.

The Hatter shook his head mournfully. "Not I!" he replied. "We quarreled last March—just before *he* went mad, you know—" (pointing with his tea spoon at the March Hare), "—it was at the great concert given by the Queen of Hearts, and I had to sing

> '*Twinkle, twinkle, little bat!*
> *How I wonder what you're at!*'

"You know the song, perhaps?"

"I've heard something like it," said Alice.

"It goes on, you know," the Hatter continued, "in this way:—

'Up above the world you fly,
Like a tea-tray in the sky.
Twinkle, twinkle—'

Here the Dormouse shook itself, and began singing in its sleep "Twinkle, twinkle, twinkle, twinkle—" and went on so long that they had to pinch it to make it stop.

"Well, I'd hardly finished the first verse," said the Hatter, "when the Queen jumped up and bawled out, 'He's murdering the time! Off with his head!'"

VIOLENCE.

"How dreadfully savage!" exclaimed Alice.

"And ever since that," the Hatter went on in a mournful tone, "he won't do a thing I ask! It's always six o'clock now."

time: personification.

A bright idea came into Alice's head. "Is that the reason so many tea-things are put out here?" she asked.

"Yes, that's it," said the Hatter with a sigh: "it's always tea-time, and we've no time to wash the things between whiles."

"Then you keep moving round, I suppose?" said Alice.

"Exactly so," said the Hatter: "as the things get used up."

"But what happens when you come to the beginning again?" Alice ventured to ask.

"Suppose we change the subject," the March Hare interrupted, yawning. "I'm getting tired of this. I vote the young lady tells us a story."

"I'm afraid I don't know one," said Alice, rather alarmed at the proposal.

"Then the Dormouse shall!" they both cried. "Wake up, Dormouse!" And they pinched it on both sides at once.

The Dormouse slowly opened his eyes. "I wasn't asleep," he said in a hoarse, feeble voice: "I heard every word you fellows were saying."

"Tell us a story!" said the March Hare.

"Yes, please do!" pleaded Alice.

"And be quick about it," added the Hatter, "or you'll be asleep again before it's done."

"Once upon a time there were three little sisters," the Dormouse began in a great hurry; "and their names were Elsie, Lacie, and Tillie; and they lived at the bottom of a well—"

"What did they live on?" said Alice, who always took a great interest in questions of eating and drinking.

"They lived on **treacle**," said the Dormouse, after thinking a minute or two.

treacle: molasses.

"They couldn't have done that, you know," Alice gently remarked; "they'd have been ill."

"So they were," said the Dormouse; "*very* ill."

Alice tried to fancy to herself what such an extraordinary ways of living would be like, but it puzzled her too much, so she went on: "But why did they live at the bottom of a well?"

"Take some more tea," the March Hare said to Alice, very earnestly.

"I've had nothing yet," Alice replied in an offended tone, "so I can't take more."

"You mean you can't take *less*," said the Hatter: "it's very easy to take *more* than nothing."

"Nobody asked *your* opinion," said Alice.

"Who's making personal remarks now?" the Hatter asked triumphantly.

Alice did not quite know what to say to this: so she helped herself to some tea and bread-and-butter, and then turned to the Dormouse, and repeated her question. "Why did they live at the bottom of a well?"

The Dormouse again took a minute or two to think about it, and then said, "It was a treacle-well."

"There's no such thing!" Alice was beginning very angrily, but the Hatter and the March Hare went "Sh! sh!" and the Dormouse sulkily remarked, "If you can't be civil, you'd better finish the story for yourself."

"No, please go on!" Alice said very humbly; "I won't interrupt again. I dare say there may be *one*."

"One, indeed!" said the Dormouse indignantly. However, he consented to go on. "And so these three little sisters—they were learning to draw, you know—"

"What did they draw?" said Alice, quite forgetting her promise.

"Treacle," said the Dormouse, without considering at all this time.

"I want a clean cup," interrupted the Hatter: "let's all move one place on."

He moved on as he spoke, and the Dormouse followed him: the March Hare moved into the Dormouse's place, and Alice rather unwillingly took the place of the March Hare. The Hatter was the only one who got any advantage from the change: and Alice was a good deal worse off than before, as the March Hare had just upset the milk-jug into his plate.

Alice did not wish to offend the Dormouse again, so she began very cautiously: "But I don't understand. Where did they draw the treacle from?"

"You can draw water out of a water-well," said the Hatter; "so I should think you could draw treacle out of a treacle-well—eh, stupid?"

"But they were *in* the well," Alice said to the Dormouse, not choosing to notice this last remark.

"Of course they were," said the Dormouse; "—**well in**."

well in: a slang expression meaning very tired.

This answer so confused poor Alice, that she let the Dormouse go on for some time without interrupting it.

"They were learning to draw," the Dormouse went on, yawning and rubbing its eyes, for it was getting very sleepy; "and they drew all manner of things—everything that begins with an M—"

"Why with an M?" said Alice.

"Why not?" said the March Hare.

Alice was silent.

The Dormouse had closed its eyes by this time, and was going off into a doze; but, on being pinched by the Hatter, it woke up again with a little shriek, and went on: "—that begins with an M, such as mouse-traps, and the moon, and memory, and muchness—you know you say things are 'much of a muchness'—did you ever see such a thing as a drawing of a muchness?"

illogical.

"Really, now you ask me," said Alice, very much confused, "I don't think—"

"Then you shouldn't talk," said the Hatter.

This piece of rudeness was more than Alice could bear: she got up in great disgust, and walked off; the Dormouse fell asleep instantly, and neither of the others took the least notice of her going, though she looked back once or twice, half hoping that they would call after her: the last time she saw them, they were trying to put the Dormouse into the teapot.

obsessed with politeness.

"At any rate I'll never go *there* again!" said Alice as she picked her way through the wood. "It's the stupidest tea-party I ever was at in all my life!"

Just as she said this, she noticed that one of the trees had a door leading right into it. "That's very curious!" she thought. "But everything's curious today. I think I may as well go in at once." And in she went.

Once more she found herself in the long hall, and close to the little glass table. "Now, I'll manage better this time," she said to herself, and began by taking the little golden key, and unlocking the door that led into the garden. Then she went to work nibbling at the mushroom (she had kept a piece of it in her pocket) till she was about a foot high: then she walked down the little passage: and *then*—she found herself at last in the beautiful garden, among the bright flower-beds and the cool fountains.

COMMENTARY

In this chapter, Carroll covers epistemological (the study of the limits of knowledge) and phenomenological (the subjective study of perceptive experience) concerns. Philosophers concerned with the nature of language, such as Cambridge University philosophers Ludwig Wittgenstein and Bertrand Russell, later explored many of this chapter's themes in their works that directly attribute Carroll's *Alice* books.

The chapter begins with a nine-inch Alice approaching the March Hare's house. In front of the March Hare's home is a large table with many place settings, but the three individuals at the table are all crowded into one corner. In that corner, the March Hare and the Hatter are having tea and talking. Between them is a Dormouse, fast asleep and being used as a cushion: The March Hare and the Hatter rest their elbows on the Dormouse as they speak to each other over the Dormouse's head.

As Alice approaches the table, shouts of "No room! No room!" greet her. She counters by noting that there is plenty of room, and she sits in a large armchair. A series of contradicting statements

ensues. Alice is offered wine, but she doesn't see any on the table and is informed that, in fact, they have no wine. When she contends that offering something not available is rude, the March Hare replies that sitting down without being invited is rude of her.

The Hatter remarks to Alice that her hair needs cutting, to which Alice replies that making personal remarks is rude of him. The Hatter poses a riddle, which leads Alice to believe some fun is in store. However, each of her remarks is countered by the Hare or the Hatter in an exchange of logic riddles and wordplay that displays the imperfections of language. Alice states that she means what she says, which, she continues, is the same as saying what she means. The Hatter and the Hare disagree: The Hatter points out that the statement "I see what I eat" is not the same as "I eat what I see," and the Hare adds that the statement "I get what I like" is not the same as "I like what I get." The Dormouse, seemingly talking in his sleep, adds that the statement "I breathe when I sleep" is not the same as "I sleep when I breathe."

Alice joins the Mad Hatter, the Hare, and the Dormouse for a tea party.
Mary Evans Picture Library

When the conversation stops, Alice continues to ponder answers to the riddle that the Hatter has posed ("Why is a raven like a writing-desk?"). The Hatter, meanwhile, removes a watch from his pocket, shakes it, and asks Alice what day of the month it is. She replies the fourth, to which the Hatter responds that the watch is off by two days. The watch, it seems, isn't working correctly because the Hare attempted to lubricate it using butter. When told by the angry Hatter that butter was the wrong lubricant to use, the Hare responds that it was "the best butter," indicating that, if the quality of the butter is high the results of whatever purpose it is applied will be equally high. Of course, the Hare's reasoning is invalid. Butter (in Victorian England) is for salves and cooking; only refined oils should be used for lubricating timepieces.

The Hatter, passively conceding to the Hare's protestations concerning the butter, suggests that perhaps the watch doesn't work because the Hare failed to remove crumbs from the butter. This argument becomes moot, however, when the Mad Hatter reveals later in the chapter that Time has abandoned him altogether anyway. The Hare takes the Hatter's watch, dips it in tea, looks at it, and repeats that he used the best butter.

Looking at the watch, Alice remarks on its strangeness: It shows the day of the month, but not the time. The Hatter counters her comment by asking Alice if her watch tells her what year it is. She replies that it doesn't because years are so long that a constant reminder is not necessary. "Which is just the case with mine," answered the Hatter with a logic Alice fails to follow. She politely admits that she doesn't understand the Hatter. The Hatter, meanwhile, announces that the Dormouse is asleep again, and he pours tea upon his nose. The Dormouse shakes off the tea without opening his eyes.

The Hatter asks Alice if she has guessed the answer to the riddle. She replies that she hasn't, and the Hare and the Hatter admit they do not know the answer either. Alice sighs and informs them that they are wasting time by asking riddles that had no answers. The Hatter corrects her by asserting that matters pertaining to Time should be addressed with the pronoun "him," rather than the indirect object "it." The Hatter doubts Alice has ever spoken with Time. Alice agrees, but she adds that she has to beat time when learning music. The personal and abstract become more confused, with the Hatter speaking of Time as a person, and Alice speaking of time in the abstract sense.

However, the Hatter admits after awhile that he is not on good terms with Time. They quarreled that past March, just before the Hare went mad. The

quarrel occurred during a party given by the Queen of Hearts. The Hatter had been singing a song similar to "Twinkle, Twinkle (Little Star)" with a bat as subject instead of a star. The Dormouse interrupts the Hatter's account to Alice by singing the word "twinkle" repeatedly until he is pinched. The Hatter continues his tale, revealing that the Queen of Hearts had interrupted their quarrel and accused him of "murdering the time" (of the melody). "Off with his head!" she had shouted.

Since that occasion, "he won't do a thing I ask," relates the Hatter, referring to Time. "It's always six o'clock now." Alice reasons, and the Hatter confirms, that because it is always six o'clock, it is always teatime. Never having time to wash dishes, the tea drinkers simply move around the table when their area becomes too messy.

The Hare interrupts, demanding that Alice tell them a story. She can't think of one, so they enlist the Dormouse, who is pinched to wakefulness. The Dormouse claims he hasn't been asleep and has heard every word uttered. The Dormouse launches into a story about three sisters who lived at the bottom of a well. Alice interrupts the story, first to question what the sisters ate, then to inquire why they lived in a well.

The Hatter offers Alice more tea and initiates another logic riddle. Because Alice hasn't yet taken tea, she reasons that she can't take more. The Hatter counters that she meant she couldn't take *less,* adding that it's "very easy to take *more* than nothing." When Alice notes that she hadn't asked for his opinion, the Hatter brings the conversation back to its beginning: He points out that she is the one now guilty of making personal remarks.

At a loss, Alice takes tea and bread and butter. She repeats her question to the Dormouse about why the sisters lived in the bottom of a well. The Dormouse takes a minute or two to think about it and answers that it was a "treacle-well," because treacle was also what the sisters ate. Alice replies angrily that treacle-wells do not exist, but the Hatter and the Hare tell her to be quiet, and the Dormouse adds that he won't continue unless she acts with more civility. Alice promises not to interrupt again, but as soon as the Dormouse continues by noting the sisters were learning to draw, Alice inquires about the subjects of their drawings.

Wanting a clean cup, meanwhile, the Hatter asks everyone to move over a seat. The Hatter sits before a clean place setting, but all the others move to seats previously occupied. Alice's new place is particularly messy because the March Hare had been sitting there and recently spilled a jug of milk.

More wordplay follows after Alice encourages the Dormouse to continue his story. Alice, for example, uses the word "draw," as a verb as she wonders where the sisters drew their treacle. The Hatter points out that they drew the treacle in the same way that water is drawn from a well. Alice notes that the sisters were already in the well, and the Dormouse concurs, adding the pun that they were "well in."

Alice is confused and falls silent. The Dormouse adds that the sisters were learning to draw everything that began with the letter "M." When Alice asks why an "M," the March Hare quickly replies,

"Why not?" and Alice again falls silent. The Dormouse falls asleep in the meantime, is pinched back to wakefulness by the Hatter, and goes on to name the various things the sisters have drawn, including mousetraps, the moon, memory, and muchness.

Further confused by the list, Alice begins to scold the Dormouse: "I don't think—," she starts to say, but is interrupted by the Hatter, who asserts that one shouldn't talk when one doesn't think. Disgusted by the rude remark, Alice stands up and leaves the table. The Dormouse falls asleep, and the Hatter and March Hare resume the seats they held before Alice arrived. After walking a ways, Alice looks back and sees the Hatter and the Hare trying to put the Dormouse into a teapot.

Alice notices that a nearby tree has a door in it. Finding it very curious, and adding that "everything's curious today," Alice decides to enter through the door. She finds herself in the long hall again, close to the glass table. Being careful to follow a plan that will finally get her through the small door that opens into the wonderful garden, Alice takes the golden key from the table, unlocks the small door, takes a piece of mushroom from her pocket, and nibbles the mushroom until she is one-foot tall. She then passes into the garden.

Chapter VIII: The Queen's Croquet Ground

Alice finally enters the splendid garden she had first seen in the hall of doors. She meets the Queen of Hearts, plays a curious game of croquet, and helps the Cheshire Cat keep his head.

A large rose-tree stood near the entrance of the garden: the roses growing on it were white, but there were three gardeners at it, busily painting them red. Alice thought this a very curious thing, and she went nearer to watch them, and just as she came up to them she heard one of them say, "Look out now, Five! Don't go splashing paint over me like that!"

"I couldn't help it," said Five, in a sulky tone; "Seven jogged my elbow."

On which Seven looked up and said, "That's right, Five! Always lay the blame on others!"

"YOU'D better not talk!" said Five. "I heard the Queen say only yesterday you deserved to be beheaded!"

"What for?" said the one who had spoken first.

"That's none of *your* business, Two!" said Seven.

"Yes, it *is* his business!" said Five, "and I'll tell him—it was for bringing the cook tulip-roots instead of onions."

Seven flung down his brush, and had just begun "Well, of all the unjust things—" when his eye chanced to fall upon Alice, as she stood watching them, and he checked himself suddenly: the others looked round also, and all of them bowed low.

"Would you tell me," said Alice, a little timidly, "why you are painting those roses?"

Five and Seven said nothing, but looked at Two. Two began in a low voice, "Why the fact is, you see, Miss, this here ought to have been a *red* rose-tree, and we put a white one in by mistake; and if the Queen was to find it out, we should all

NOTES

[handwritten note: referred to by their number.]

[handwritten note: labels.]

[handwritten note: mistaken identity.]

Three playing cards paint a bush of white roses red to avoid the scorn of the Queen.
Mary Evans Picture Library

[handwritten note: weird logic]

[handwritten note: she talks to them normally. so can't be in authority]

have our heads cut off, you know. So you see, Miss, we're doing our best, afore she comes, to—" At this moment Five, who had been anxiously looking across the garden, called out "The Queen! The Queen!" and the three gardeners instantly threw themselves flat upon their faces. There was a sound of many footsteps, and Alice looked round, eager to see the Queen.

First came ten soldiers carrying clubs; these were all shaped like the three gardeners, **oblong** and flat, with their hands and feet at the corners: next the ten **courtiers**; these were ornamented all over with diamonds, and walked two and two, as the soldiers did. After these came the royal children; there were ten of them, and the little dears came jumping merrily along hand in hand, in couples: they were all ornamented with hearts. Next came the guests, mostly Kings and Queens, and among them Alice recognized the White Rabbit: it was talking in a hurried nervous manner, smiling at everything that was said, and went by without noticing her. Then followed the Knave of Hearts, carrying the King's crown on a crimson velvet cushion; and, last of all this grand procession, came THE KING AND QUEEN OF HEARTS. Alice was rather doubtful whether she ought not to lie down on her face like the three gardeners, but she could not remember ever having heard of such a rule at processions; 'and besides, what would be the use of a procession,' thought she, 'if people had all to lie down upon their faces, so that they couldn't see it?' So she stood still where she was, and waited.

When the procession came opposite to Alice, they all stopped and looked at her, and the Queen said severely "Who is this?" She said it to the **Knave of Hearts**, who only bowed and smiled in reply.

oblong: longer than broad; elongated.

courtiers: an attendant at a royal court.

Knave of Hearts: a male servant; in this instance, the Jack of Hearts.

[handwritten margin notes:]

King is more important.
Queen has more power.

manners.

servants: lower etc.

"Idiot!" said the Queen, tossing her head impatiently; and, turning to Alice, she went on, "What's your name, child?"

"My name is Alice, so please your Majesty," said Alice very politely; but she added, to herself, "Why, they're only a pack of cards, after all. I needn't be afraid of them!"

"And who are *these*?" said the Queen, pointing to the three gardeners who were lying round the rose-tree; for, you see, as they were lying on their faces, and the pattern on their backs was the same as the rest of the pack, she could not tell whether they were gardeners, or soldiers, or courtiers, or three of her own children.

"How should I know?" said Alice, surprised at her own courage. "It's no business of *mine*."

The Queen turned crimson with fury, and, after glaring at her for a moment like a wild beast, screamed "Off with her head! Off—"

"Nonsense!" said Alice, very loudly and decidedly, and the Queen was silent.

The King laid his hand upon her arm, and timidly said "Consider, my dear: she is only a child!"

The Queen turned angrily away from him, and said to the Knave "Turn them over!"

The Knave did so, very carefully, with one foot.

"Get up!" said the Queen, in a shrill, loud voice, and the three gardeners instantly jumped up, and began bowing to the King, the Queen, the royal children, and everybody else.

"Leave off that!" screamed the Queen. "You make me giddy." And then turning to the rose-tree, she went on, "What *have* you been doing here?"

"May it please your Majesty," said Two, in a very humble tone, going down on one knee as he spoke, "we were trying—"

[handwritten margin notes:] defying convention of queen.

→ starts very politely.

rudeness. more assertive than at the beginning

"I see!" said the Queen, who had meanwhile been examining the roses. "Off with their heads!" and the procession moved on, three of the soldiers remaining behind to execute the unfortunate gardeners, who ran to Alice for protection.

"You shan't be beheaded!" said Alice, and she put them into a large flower-pot that stood near. The three soldiers wandered about for a minute or two, looking for them, and then quietly marched off after the others.

"Are their heads off?" shouted the Queen.

"Their heads are gone, if it please your Majesty!" the soldiers shouted in reply.

"That's right!" shouted the Queen. "Can you play croquet?"

The soldiers were silent, and looked at Alice, as the question was evidently meant for her.

"Yes!" shouted Alice.

"Come on, then!" roared the Queen, and Alice joined the procession, wondering very much what would happen next.

"It's—it's a very fine day!" said a timid voice at her side. She was walking by the White Rabbit, who was peeping anxiously into her face.

"Very," said Alice: "—where's the Duchess?"

"Hush! Hush!" said the Rabbit in a low, hurried tone. He looked anxiously over his shoulder as he spoke, and then raised himself upon tiptoe, put his mouth close to her ear, and whispered "She's under sentence of execution."

"What for?" said Alice.

"Did you say 'What a pity!'?" the Rabbit asked.

"No, I didn't," said Alice: "I don't think it's at all a pity. I said, 'What for?'"

"She boxed the Queen's ears—" the Rabbit began. Alice gave a little scream of laughter. "Oh, hush!" the Rabbit whispered in a frightened

[handwritten margin notes:]
Alice is a figure of authority.
Alice is opposed to the violence.
everyone shouting chaos.
morbid
expects politeness
language change

tone. "The Queen will hear you! You see, she came rather late, and the Queen said—"

"Get to your places!" shouted the Queen in a voice of thunder, and people began running about in all directions, tumbling up against each other; however, they got settled down in a minute or two, and the game began. Alice thought she had never seen such a curious croquet-ground in her life; it was all ridges and furrows; the balls were live **hedgehogs**, the **mallets** live **flamingoes**, and the soldiers had to double themselves up and to stand on their hands and feet, to make the **arches**. The chief difficulty Alice found at first was in managing her flamingo: she succeeded in getting its body tucked away, comfortably enough, under her arm, with its legs hanging down, but generally, just as she had got its neck nicely straightened out, and was going to give the hedgehog a blow with its head, it *would* twist itself round and look up in her face, with such a puzzled expression that she could not help bursting out laughing: and when she had got its head down, and was going to begin again, it was very provoking to find that the hedgehog had unrolled itself, and was in the act of crawling away: besides all this, there was generally a ridge or furrow in the way wherever she wanted to send the hedgehog to, and, as the doubled-up soldiers were always getting up and walking off to other parts of the ground, Alice soon came to the conclusion that it was a very difficult game indeed.

The players all played at once without waiting for turns, quarrelling all the while, and fighting for the hedgehogs; and in a very short time the Queen was in a furious passion, and went stamping about, and shouting "Off with his head!" or "Off with her head!" about once in a minute.

hedgehog: any of several small insectivores of the Old World, with a shaggy coat and sharp spines on the back, which bristle and form a defense when the animal curls up.

mallet: a long-handled hammer, usually with a cylindrical wooden head, used in playing croquet.

flamingo: any of the order of large, tropical birds with long legs, webbed feet, long necks, downward-curving beaks, and bright pink or red feathers.

arches: the hoops that the croquet balls (hedgehogs) are supposed to be hit through.

Alice struggles to play croquet using a flamingo for a mallet and a hedgehog for a croquet ball.
Mary Evans Picture Library

Alice began to feel very uneasy: to be sure, she had not as yet had any dispute with the Queen, but she knew that it might happen any minute, "and then," thought she, "what would become of me? They're dreadfully fond of beheading people here; the great wonder is, that there's any one left alive!" She was looking about for some way of escape, and wondering whether she could get away without being seen, when she noticed a curious appearance in the air: it puzzled her very much at first, but, after watching it a minute or two, she made it out to be a grin, and she said to herself 'It's the Cheshire Cat: now I shall have somebody to talk to.'

"How are you getting on?" said the Cat, as soon as there was mouth enough for it to speak with. Alice waited till the eyes appeared, and then nodded. "It's no use speaking to it," she thought, "till its ears have come, or at least one of them." In another minute the whole head appeared, and then Alice put down her flamingo, and began an account of the game, feeling very glad she had someone to listen to her. The Cat seemed to think that there was enough of it now in sight, and no more of it appeared.

"I don't think they play at all fairly," Alice began, in rather a complaining tone, "and they all quarrel so dreadfully one can't hear oneself speak—and they don't seem to have any rules in particular; at least, if there are, nobody attends to them—and you've no idea how confusing it is all the things being alive; for instance, there's the arch I've got to go through next walking about at the other end of the ground—and I should have croqueted the Queen's hedgehog just now, only it ran away when it saw mine coming!"

"How do you like the Queen?" said the Cat in a low voice.

"Not at all," said Alice: "she's so extremely—" Just then she noticed that the Queen was close behind her, listening: so she went on, "—likely to win, that it's hardly worth while finishing the game." The Queen smiled and passed on.

read carefully around he.

"Who *are* you talking to?" said the King, going up to Alice, and looking at the Cat's head with great curiosity.

"It's a friend of mine—a Cheshire Cat," said Alice: "allow me to introduce it."

→ doesn't have an identity

"I don't like the look of it at all," said the King: "however, it may kiss my hand if it likes."

→ arrogant.

"I'd rather not," the Cat remarked.

"Don't be impertinent," said the King, "and don't look at me like that!" He got behind Alice as he spoke.

→ Alice & cheshire cat are the only ones who stand up the Authority.

"A cat may look at a king," said Alice. "I've read that in some book, but I don't remember where."

"Well, it must be removed," said the King very decidedly, and he called the Queen, who was passing at the moment, "My dear! I wish you would have this cat removed!"

→ "if its any trouble- just remove it.

The Queen had only one way of settling all difficulties, great or small. "Off with his head!" she said, without even looking round.

"I'll fetch the executioner myself," said the King eagerly, and he hurried off.

the Cat is very ~~not~~ impertinant : unlike the

Alice thought she might as well go back, and see how the game was going on, as she heard the Queen's voice in the distance, screaming with passion. She had already heard her sentence three of the players to be executed for having missed their turns, and she did not like the look of things at all, as the game was in such confusion that she never knew whether it was her turn or not. So she went in search of her hedgehog. The hedgehog was engaged in a fight with another hedgehog, which seemed to Alice an

Cat : maybe God ???

excellent opportunity for **croqueting** one of them with the other: the only difficulty was, that her flamingo was gone across to the other side of the garden, where Alice could see it trying in a helpless sort of way to fly up into a tree.

By the time she had caught the flamingo and brought it back, the fight was over, and both the hedgehogs were out of sight: "but it doesn't matter much," thought Alice, "as all the arches are gone from this side of the ground." So she tucked it away under her arm, that it might not escape again, and went back for a little more conversation with her friend.

When she got back to the Cheshire Cat, she was surprised to find quite a large crowd collected round it: there was a dispute going on between the executioner, the King, and the Queen, who were all talking at once, while all the rest were quite silent, and looked very uncomfortable.

The moment Alice appeared, she was appealed to by all three to settle the question, and they repeated their arguments to her, though, as they all spoke at once, she found it very hard indeed to make out exactly what they said.

The executioner's argument was, that you couldn't cut off a head unless there was a body to cut it off from: that he had never had to do such a thing before, and he wasn't going to begin at *his* time of life.

The King's argument was, that anything that had a head could be beheaded, and that you weren't to talk nonsense.

The Queen's argument was, that if something wasn't done about it in less than no time she'd have everybody executed, all round. (It was this last remark that had made the whole party look so grave and anxious.)

[handwritten margin notes:] all futile, all pointless.

Queen & King are actually very stupid.

seems illogical. but

Alice could think of nothing else to say but "It belongs to the Duchess: you'd better ask *her* about it."

"She's in prison," the Queen said to the executioner: "fetch her here." And the executioner went off like an arrow. → *they all obey her.*

The Cat's head began fading away the moment he was gone, and, by the time he had come back with the Dutchess, it had entirely disappeared; so the King and the executioner ran wildly up and down looking for it, while the rest of the party went back to the game.

COMMENTARY

In this chapter, Carroll introduces the violently temperamental Queen of Hearts who incessantly orders executions. Alice plays an absurd, nonsensical game of croquet with the King and Queen of Hearts where mallets and balls are substituted with flamingoes and hedgehogs. The absence of rules in the playing of the game masks one truth, which is that the Queen or the King must be determined the winner. Through this game, Carroll may be taking a satirical swipe at the tilting of rules in Victorian England to favor the aristocracy.

The chapter begins with Alice entering the garden and approaching a large rose tree. Alice had been longing to reach the garden since she first spied it. She had a romantic view of it, but immediately upon actually entering the garden she discovers that it is a corrupt place. For example, the flowers of the rose tree are naturally white, but three gardeners are in the process of painting them red. Each of the gardeners has a body similar to a playing card. Thus, they are two-dimensional—like most other characters she will encounter in the garden. Alice overhears one of the gardeners tell another, named Five, to stop splashing paint on him. Five claims that Seven has bumped into him, to which Seven remarks

that Five always lays blame on others. Five counters by claiming that yesterday he heard the Queen say that Seven ought to be beheaded. The threat of violence is another element of corruption in the garden. Alice interrupts their argument by asking why the gardeners are painting the roses.

Two explains to Alice that the gardeners were supposed to have planted a red rose tree and they are trying to correct their mistake before the Queen notices. The Queen would have their heads chopped off for the mistake. Five cries out that the Queen is approaching. The gardeners lay face down on the ground, but Alice turns around to look.

A procession of two-dimensional characters comes their way, led by ten soldiers walking two abreast and carrying clubs. They are followed by ten courtiers all wearing diamonds. Ten royal children, ornamented with hearts, run along next, two at a time, followed by guests, including the White Rabbit. As he has done the previous times Alice saw him, the White Rabbit is speaking hurriedly and nervously. The Knave of Hearts carries the King's crown, and the King and Queen of Hearts are at the end of the procession.

The procession stops when the Queen spots Alice and asks the Knave of Hearts, "Who is this?" After the Knave simply bows and smiles, the Queen addresses Alice directly. Alice is unafraid and says her name to the Queen. The Queen asks her about the three gardeners lying on the ground. Their backs have the same pattern as everyone else in the pack. "How should I know?" Alice replies flippantly. "It's no business of *mine*."

The Queen becomes furious at this flippancy toward her authority and screams, "Off with her head!" Before she can repeat the phrase a second time, Alice responds, "Nonsense!" rejecting the statement. Crying "nonsense!" is a way for Alice to reject threats to herself and her identity while in Wonderland. The King requests that the Queen consider the fact that Alice is only a child. His identifying Alice as "only a child" suggests that the King and Queen are adult and perhaps parental figures. The Queen turns her attention to the gardeners and orders the Knave to turn them over. The Queen compels the gardeners to rise. The gardeners comply and begin bowing to everyone present. The Queen orders them to stop bowing and inquires as to what they have been doing.

Before they can explain, the Queen summarily responds, "*I see*," and commands their beheading. This is another of several instances in Wonderland where a conclusion or a verdict is reached before information can be presented. Three soldiers remain behind to supervise the execution while the procession moves on. The gardeners run to Alice for protection, and she assures them they won't be executed. She hides them. The Queen shouts back to the soldiers, asking if the gardeners' heads were off. The soldiers reply that the gardeners' heads were gone, satisfying the Queen even though they meant the word "gone" differently (as in "out of sight") than the Queen interpreted it (as in "detached from the neck"). Words are being used

deceptively in this case to project an alternate reality. Then the Queen shouts out the question, "Can you play croquet?" When the soldiers remain silent, Alice realizes the question is meant for her.

Alice affirms that she can play croquet and she joins the procession. She soon finds that she is walking next to the White Rabbit. Alice asks the White Rabbit about the Duchess she had met who had been invited by the Queen to play croquet. The Rabbit hushes her while he looks anxiously over his shoulder back at the Queen. He whispers to Alice that the Duchess is under sentence of execution for having boxed the Queen's ears. The Rabbit is about to explain the incident when the Queen shouts out, "Get to your places!" A mad scramble ensues.

The croquet game is the most curious one that Alice has ever seen. The field has ridges and furrows rather than a relatively flat surface, hedgehogs take the place of croquet balls, flamingoes serve as mallets, and wickets are formed by soldiers who double over. Managing the flamingo as a mallet is difficult: Alice has to hold the long-legged bird and straighten its neck, but before she can use the flamingo's head to hit a hedgehog, the neck twists away. Meanwhile, the hedgehogs unroll and move on by themselves, and the doubled-up soldiers frequently change places. Much like the Caucus-race, all the players play simultaneously, without taking turns. Games are usually governed by rules, but in Wonderland, games are chaotic. By trying to make sense of such activities, Alice reflects the attempts of people to find order in an ever-changing reality. During the game, the Queen runs about ordering executions. The arbitrariness of her behavior is another form of disorder in the chaotic garden. Alice begins to fear for her own head, even though she hasn't done anything wrong.

Alice is looking around for a way to escape when she notices a curious appearance in the air.

Alice attempts to hit a croquet ball (a hedgehog) with her mallet (a flamingo) as the King and Queen look on.
The Everett Collection

After awhile she makes it out to be the grin of the Cheshire Cat. The Cat asks her how she is doing, but Alice waits until his ears have faded in so that the Cat can hear her. Alice assumes that the Cat won't hear her unless his ears are within view. The idea that the Cat may be entirely present at the moment with only parts of him invisible (which would not, necessarily, render them inoperable) does not occur to her.

Alice puts down her flamingo and describes the game to the Cat. She complains about the lack of rules and the confusion and unfairness of playing with live balls, mallets, and wickets. What Alice fails to realize, however, is that a game without rules cannot be played fairly or unfairly. It can only be played with no external qualifications placed upon it. Because adults, led by the King and Queen, govern the game, Carroll here exposes the fallibility of the adult world. Significantly, the child Alice and several animals—the flamingoes and hedgehogs who do not conform to the roles expected of them, and the Cheshire Cat—defy the imposed reality of the adults. They can be seen as representing dynamic forms of life, while the Queen, with her incessant calls for execution, represents death.

When the Cat asks Alice how she likes the Queen, Alice begins by saying "Not at all, she's so extremely—" before she notices the Queen behind her, listening. Alice finishes by saying "likely to win." Of course, Alice is merely saying what she knows the Queen wants to hear. Satisfied with the answer, the Queen moves on. The King comes along to ask with whom Alice was speaking, and Alice introduces him to the Cheshire Cat. The King remarks that he doesn't like the look of the Cat, but he adds that the Cat is allowed to kiss his hand. The Cat refuses. Wanting the Cat removed for insolence, the King appeals to the Queen, who shouts "Off with his head!" The humor of such a statement lies, of course, in the fact that the Cat exists *only* as a head. To behead it is a linguistic impossibility as one would need to remove the head from a body to say that it is beheaded. If the creature has no body, it cannot be beheaded.

Alice returns to the game. While noticing the Queen off in the distance screaming, Alice retrieves her flamingo, but she can't find her hedgehog. When she returns to the Cheshire Cat she finds a crowd gathered beneath him. The King, the Queen, and the Executioner are arguing, and when Alice appears, they all at once appeal to her to settle the issue. The Executioner explains a metaphysical conundrum that one can't cut off a head if it is not attached to a body, referring to the Cat whose suspended head is the only part of his body visible in the sky. The King argues that anything with a head can be beheaded. The Queen states simply that unless the issue is resolved, everyone will be beheaded. The only options for life in this garden world seem to be death or a metaphysical quandary. The fraud of the Queen's threat—utter annihilation—and the failure of reason are exposed by the Cat's appearance.

The Queen orders the beheading of the Cheshire Cat.
Mary Evans Picture Library

Alice notes that the Cat belongs to the Duchess, and she feels that the Duchess should make the decision. The Duchess is summoned from prison. In her earlier appearance, the Duchess was a moralizer, among other things, and it is significant that a moralizer should be called to help resolve an issue where chaos (metaphysical quandary) and death are seemingly the only possible realities in life. Meanwhile, the Cat's head fades from view. The chapter ends with the King and the Executioner searching for the Cat while everyone else resumes the game of croquet.

Chapter IX: The Mock Turtle's Story

Alice is befriended by the moralizing Duchess, is taken by a Gryphon to meet the Mock Turtle, and hears the sad and solemn Mock Turtle tell of his schooling in the sea.

"You can't think how glad I am to see you again, you dear old thing!" said the Duchess, as she tucked her arm affectionately into Alice's, and they walked off together.

Alice was very glad to find her in such a pleasant temper, and thought to herself that perhaps it was only the pepper that had made her so savage when they met in the kitchen.

"When *I'm* a Duchess," she said to herself, (not in a very hopeful tone though), "I won't have any pepper in my kitchen *at all*. Soup does very well without—Maybe it's always pepper that makes people hot-tempered," she went on, very much pleased at having found out a new kind of rule, "and vinegar that makes them sour—and **camomile** that makes them bitter—and—and **barley-sugar** and such things that make children sweet-tempered. I only wish people knew that: then they wouldn't be so stingy about it, you know—"

She had quite forgotten the Duchess by this time, and was a little startled when she heard her voice close to her ear. "You're thinking about something, my dear, and that makes you forget to talk. I can't tell you just now what the moral of that is, but I shall remember it in a bit."

"Perhaps it hasn't one," Alice ventured to remark.

"Tut, tut, child!" said the Duchess. "Everything's got a moral, if only you can find it." And she squeezed herself up closer to Alice's side as she spoke.

Alice did not much like keeping so close to her: first, because the Duchess was *very* ugly; and

NOTES

Duchess: illogical.

has aspirations for herself

camomile: a plant whose dried, daisylike flower heads are used as a medicine and in making tea.

barley-sugar: a clear, hard candy made by melting sugar, formerly with a barley extract added.

why does wonderland have morals.

Duchess isn't biding by the social rules.

secondly, because she was exactly the right height to rest her chin upon Alice's shoulder, and it was an uncomfortably sharp chin. However, she did not like to be rude, so she bore it as well as she could.

suffering in silence.

social manners.

"The game's going on rather better now," she said, by way of keeping up the conversation a little.

"'Tis so," said the Duchess: "and the moral of that is—'Oh, 'tis love, 'tis love, that makes the world go round!'"

"Somebody said," Alice whispered, "that it's done by everybody minding their own business!"

"Ah, well! It means much the same thing," said the Duchess, digging her sharp little chin into Alice's shoulder as she added, "and the moral of *that* is — 'Take care of the sense, and the sounds will take care of themselves.'"

"How fond she is of finding morals in things!" Alice thought to herself.

"I dare say you're wondering why I don't put my arm round your waist," the Duchess said after a pause: "the reason is, that I'm doubtful about the temper of your flamingo. Shall I try the experiment?"

"*He* might bite," Alice cautiously replied, not feeling at all anxious to have the experiment tried.

"Very true," said the Duchess: "flamingoes and mustard both bite. And the moral of that is — 'Birds of a feather flock together.'"

"Only mustard isn't a bird," Alice remarked.

"Right, as usual," said the Duchess: "what a clear way you have of putting things!"

"It's a mineral, I *think*," said Alice.

"Of course it is," said the Duchess, who seemed ready to agree to everything that Alice said;

"there's a large mustard-mine near here. And the

moral of that is—'The more there is of mine, the less there is of yours.'"

"Oh, I know!" exclaimed Alice, who had not attended to this last remark, "it's a vegetable. It doesn't look like one, but it is."

"I quite agree with you," said the Duchess; "and the moral of that is — 'Be what you would seem to be'—or if you'd like it put more simply— 'Never imagine yourself not to be otherwise than what it might appear to others that what you were or might have been was not otherwise than what you had been would have appeared to them to be otherwise.'"

"I think I should understand that better," Alice said very politely, "if I had it written down: but I can't quite follow it as you say it."

"That's nothing to what I could say if I chose," the Duchess replied, in a pleased tone.

"Pray don't trouble yourself to say it any longer than that," said Alice.

pleased to have confused her.

"Oh, don't talk about trouble!" said the Duchess. "I make you a present of everything I've said as yet."

"A cheap sort of present!" thought Alice. "I'm glad they don't give birthday presents like that!" But she did not venture to say it out loud.

"Thinking again?" the Duchess asked, with another dig of her sharp little chin.

"I've a right to think," said Alice sharply, for she was beginning to feel a little worried.

"Just about as much right," said the Duchess, "as pigs have to fly; and the m—"

But here, to Alice's great surprise, the Duchess's voice died away, even in the middle of her favourite word "moral," and the arm that was linked into hers began to tremble. Alice looked up, and there stood the Queen in front of them, with her arms folded, frowning like a thunderstorm.

"A fine day, your Majesty!" the Duchess began in a low, weak voice.

"Now, I give you fair warning," shouted the Queen, stamping on the ground as she spoke; "either you or your head must be off, and that in about half no time! Take your choice!"

The Duchess took her choice, and was gone in a moment.

"Let's go on with the game," the Queen said to Alice; and Alice was too much frightened to say a word, but slowly followed her back to the croquet-ground.

The other guests had taken advantage of the Queen's absence, and were resting in the shade: however, the moment they saw her, they hurried back to the game, the Queen merely remarking that a moment's delay would cost them their lives.

All the time they were playing the Queen never left off quarrelling with the other players, and shouting "Off with his head!" or "Off with her head!" Those whom she sentenced were taken into custody by the soldiers, who of course had to leave off being arches to do this, so that by the end of half an hour or so there were no arches left, and all the players, except the King, the Queen, and Alice, were in custody and under sentence of execution.

Then the Queen left off, quite out of breath, and said to Alice, "Have you seen the **Mock Turtle** yet?"

"No," said Alice. "I don't even know what a Mock Turtle is."

"It's the thing Mock Turtle Soup is made from," said the Queen.

"I never saw one, or heard of one," said Alice.

"Come on, then," said the Queen, "and he shall tell you his history."

mock turtle: a substitute, usually a calf's head or veal, used in making mock turtle soup.

associates play on words with real animal.

As they walked off together, Alice heard the King say in a low voice, to the company generally, "You are all pardoned." "Come, *that's* a good thing!" she said to herself, for she had felt quite unhappy at the number of executions the Queen had ordered.

They very soon came upon a **Gryphon**, lying fast asleep in the sun. (*If* you don't know what a Gryphon is, look at the picture.) "Up, lazy thing!" said the Queen, "and take this young lady to see the Mock Turtle, and to hear his history. I must go back and see after some executions I have ordered"; and she walked off, leaving Alice alone with the Gryphon. Alice did not quite like the look of the creature, but on the whole she thought it would be quite as safe to stay with it as to go after that savage Queen: so she waited.

The Gryphon sat up and rubbed its eyes: then it watched the Queen till she was out of sight: then it chuckled. "What fun!" said the Gryphon, half to itself, half to Alice.

"What *is* the fun?" said Alice.

"Why, *she,*" said the Gryphon. "It's all her fancy, that: they never executes nobody, you know. Come on!"

"Everybody says 'come on!' here," thought Alice, as she went slowly after it: "I never was so ordered about in all my life, never!"

They had not gone far before they saw the Mock Turtle in the distance, sitting sad and lonely on a little ledge of rock, and, as they came nearer, Alice could hear him sighing as if his heart would break. She pitied him deeply. "What is his sorrow?" she asked the Gryphon, and the Gryphon answered, very nearly in the same words as before, "It's all his fancy, that: he hasn't got no sorrow, you know. Come on!"

The Gryphon resting under a tree.
Mary Evans Picture Library

gryphon: a mythical monster with the body and hind legs of a lion, and the head, wings, and claws of an eagle.

So they went up to the Mock Turtle, who looked at them with large eyes full of tears, but said nothing.

"This here young lady," said the Gryphon, "she wants for to know your history, she do."

"I'll tell it her," said the Mock Turtle in a deep, hollow tone: "sit down, both of you, and don't speak a word till I've finished."

So they sat down, and nobody spoke for some minutes. Alice thought to herself, "I don't see how he can *even* finish, if he doesn't begin." But she waited patiently.

"Once," said the Mock Turtle at last, with a deep sigh, "I was a real Turtle."

These words were followed by a very long silence, broken only by an occasional exclamation of "Hjckrrh!" from the Gryphon, and the constant heavy sobbing of the Mock Turtle. Alice was very nearly getting up and saying, "Thank you, sir, for your interesting story," but she could not help thinking there *must* be more to come, so she sat still and said nothing.

"When we were little," the Mock Turtle went on at last, more calmly, though still sobbing a little now and then, "we went to school in the sea. The master was an old Turtle—we used to call him Tortoise—"

"Why did you call him Tortoise, if he wasn't one?" Alice asked.

"**We called him Tortoise because he taught us**," said the Mock Turtle angrily: "really you are very dull!"

"You ought to be ashamed of yourself for asking such a simple question," added the Gryphon; and then they both sat silent and looked at poor Alice, who felt ready to sink into the earth. At last the Gryphon said to the Mock Turtle, "Drive

"We called him Tortoise because he taught us:" a pun on the word "tortoise," which is how the Turtle pronounces "taught us."

on, old fellow! Don't be all day about it!" and he went on in these words:

"Yes, we went to school in the sea, though you mayn't believe it—"

"I never said I didn't!" interrupted Alice.

"You did," said the Mock Turtle.

"Hold your tongue!" added the Gryphon, before Alice could speak again. The Mock Turtle went on.

"We had the best of educations—in fact, we went to school every day—"

"I'VE been to a day school, too," said Alice; "you needn't be so proud as all that."

"With extras?" asked the Mock Turtle a little anxiously.

"Yes," said Alice, "we learned French and music."

"And washing?" said the Mock Turtle.

"Certainly not!" said Alice indignantly.

"Ah! then yours wasn't a really good school," said the Mock Turtle in a tone of great relief. "Now at *ours* they had at the end of the bill, 'French, music, *and washing*—extra.'"

"You couldn't have wanted it much," said Alice; "living at the bottom of the sea."

"I couldn't afford to learn it." said the Mock Turtle with a sigh. "I only took the regular course."

"What was that?" inquired Alice.

"**Reeling and Writhing**, of course, to begin with," the Mock Turtle replied; "and then the different branches of Arithmetic—Ambition, Distraction, Uglification, and Derision."

"I never heard of 'Uglification,'" Alice ventured to say. "What is it?"

The Gryphon lifted up both its paws in surprise. "What! Never heard of uglifying!" it exclaimed. "You know what to beautify is, I suppose?"

"Yes," said Alice doubtfully: "it means—to—make—anything—prettier."

> *"Reeling and Writhing:"* a malapropism of Reading and Writing

[handwritten note:] malapropism: using wrong word with context.

"Well, then," the Gryphon went on, "if you don't know what to uglify is, you *are* a simpleton." Alice did not feel encouraged to ask any more questions about it, so she turned to the Mock Turtle, and said "What else had you to learn?"

"Well, there was Mystery," the Mock Turtle replied, counting off the subjects on his flappers, "—Mystery, ancient and modern, with Seaography: then Drawling—the Drawling-master was an old conger-eel, that used to come once a week: *he* taught us Drawling, Stretching, and Fainting in Coils."

"What was *that* like?" said Alice.

"Well, I can't show it you myself," the Mock Turtle said: "I'm too stiff. And the Gryphon never learnt it."

"Hadn't time," said the Gryphon: "I went to the Classics master, though. He was an old crab, he was."

"I never went to him," the Mock Turtle said with a sigh: "he taught Laughing and Grief, they used to say."

"So he did, so he did," said the Gryphon, sighing in his turn; and both creatures hid their faces in their paws.

"And how many hours a day did you do lessons?" said Alice, in a hurry to change the subject.

"Ten hours the first day," said the Mock Turtle: "nine the next, and so on."

"What a curious plan!" exclaimed Alice.

"That's the reason they're called lessons," the Gryphon remarked: "because they lessen from day to day."

This was quite a new idea to Alice, and she thought it over a little before she made her next remark. "Then the eleventh day must have been a holiday?"

actually a crab: or could be a bastard.

"Of course it was," said the Mock Turtle.

"And how did you manage on the twelfth?" Alice went on eagerly.

"That's enough about lessons," the Gryphon interrupted in a very decided tone: "tell her something about the games now."

COMMENTARY

Chapter IX continues Carroll's exploration of logical conclusions developed from faulty propositions and wordplay. The former is evidenced by Alice's reencounter with the Duchess, who makes broad speculative generalizations, which she calls morals, about nearly everything she and Alice discuss. The moralizing Duchess is a parody of adult characters of popular children's books of the nineteenth century, where young characters typically have frightful adventures and learn lessons about life from adults. The Red Queen introduces Alice to the Gryphon. The Gryphon takes Alice to meet the Mock Turtle, an inventively playful name for an animal who makes the best puns in either of the *Wonderland* books.

When the chapter begins, the Duchess appears and greets Alice affectionately. They walk together arm in arm. Alice notes that the Duchess seems in a much better mood than during their last encounter in the kitchen, when she was mean to the baby that turned into a pig. Perhaps the pepper had made her savage back then, thinks Alice. Alice imagines that when she herself becomes a Duchess she will not allow pepper in her kitchen. Alice goes on to consider whether pepper is the source of all evil temper. Pleased at "having found out a new kind of rule," Alice wonders whether vinegar might be the source of sour moods, chamomile the source of bitterness, and barley-sugar a source of sweet moods. Of course, this

approach is untrue, but Alice hasn't the chance to share her theory with the Duchess who, no doubt, would've agreed with her. Like many in Wonderland, Alice uses logic to derive an absurd conclusion from a faulty premise. After a faulty proposition is advanced, characters develop it to comical conclusions.

The Duchess notices that Alice is silent and attributes it to the fact that she must be thinking about something. Thinking about something makes one forget to talk, observes the Duchess, but she admits to being at a loss as to the moral of the statement. When Alice suggests that perhaps the statement has no moral, the Duchess replies, "everything's got a moral." The Duchess first says that silence implies deep thought, which, of course, is an assumption arrived at erroneously. Second, the Duchess assumes that every statement implies a more broad truth, which, again, is in error.

Alice feels uncomfortable and threatened by the Duchess' physical demands: She places herself uncomfortably close to Alice, digs her pointed chin into Alice's shoulder, and makes an attempt to place her arm around Alice's waist. Only the presence of the flamingo in Alice's other arm foils this maneuver, and Alice warns the Duchess that the flamingo might bite her if she proceeds too far. It is interesting to note that John Tenniel's illustrations of the hideously ugly Duchess forego a pointed chin as noted in Carroll's text. Instead, Tenniel's rendering of the Duchess, ugly as she is, features a squared-off chin, perhaps due to an actual acquaintance or intended model that Tenniel used for his vision of an unattractive woman.

Alice remarks on the croquet game, which seems to be progressing better. The Duchess agrees and provides a moral: "'tis love that makes the world go round!" Of course, the moral is ridiculous, as the croquet game has nothing to do with the earth's rotation; nor does love have anything to do with the croquet game. Recalling what the Duchess said to her back in her kitchen, Alice repeats that she was told by someone (the Duchess) that the world goes round by everyone minding their own business. The Duchess agrees and adds another moral to her previous moral, "Take care of the sense, and the sounds will take care of themselves." This reflects her previous statement concerning Alice's thoughts and that those thoughts cause Alice to be silent. After Alice thinks through her ideas, the Duchess seems to be saying, anything she says is rife with significance. Of course, being a little girl, Alice simply is not capable of producing a verbal gem each time she opens her mouth.

Concerned about the flamingo in Alice's other arm, the Duchess observes that flamingoes and mustard both bite—the moral being that birds of a feather flock together. Alice replies that mustard isn't a bird; she believes it is a mineral. The agreeable Duchess observes that there is a mustard mine nearby and offers another moral, but Alice remembers that mustard is a vegetable, to which the Duchess agrees and adds several more morals. In this, the Duchess employs the logic of the syllogism—where one truthful statement is

combined with a second to form a general truth—when the meanings of the words are entirely different. In the case of the flamingo, the verb "bite" is literal. The "bite" of mustard metaphorically implies the seed's tangy attributes.

Alice tries to remain polite. The Duchess offers her as a gift all the morals she has recently related. Alice thinks it a cheap gift and is glad that birthday presents are better. The conversation ends when the two encounter the Queen. She is standing before them and "frowning like a thunderstorm."

The Duchess greets the Queen pleasantly, but the Queen warns the Duchess that either she must leave or her head must be cut off. The Duchess leaves. The Queen invites Alice to continue the game of croquet, and then she resumes ordering executions. Soldiers are leaving their posts as wickets to take away those who are to be executed. Soon, no wickets remain because all of the players except for the Queen, King, and Alice have been taken into custody.

The Queen advises Alice to see the Mock Turtle and leads her away in the direction of the Turtle. When the Queen leaves, the King pardons all those scheduled for beheading. In this garden where rules of croquet are chaotic and the Queen threatens beheading for even the slightest mistake or offense, the King's sweeping pardons are yet another example of arbitrariness: Even justice is arbitrary or irrational.

The Queen leads Alice to a Gryphon, a mythological monster who, nevertheless, sports a lower-class British accent. The Queen awakens the Gryphon and orders him to take Alice to the Mock Turtle. The Gryphon watches the Queen leave and exclaims, "What fun!," adding that no one ever really gets executed in Wonderland. The terrifying threat of Wonderland is proven to be illusory or unreal.

The Mock Turtle is sitting on a rock and sighing deeply when Alice and the Gryphon arrive. Alice inquires about the reason for the Mock Turtle's sorrow, and the Gryphon answers ungrammatically that it's his fancy, "he hasn't got no sorrows." He has also called the Queen's habit of ordering executions a fancy. This statement may indicate Carroll's observation that various individuals adopt the habits and faults or flaws of others as an easy substitute for personal identity. For example, the Queen seems to define her identity (and authority) by her ability to order executions. The Mock Turtle, one of the few characters in Wonderland to show genuine emotion, represents another extreme—excessive sentimentality.

The Gryphon introduces Alice to the Mock Turtle as someone interested in hearing his history. The Mock Turtle orders them both to sit and remain quiet. After a long silence, the Mock Turtle begins his story by saying, "Once, I was a real Turtle." Another spell of silence ensues, except for an occasional exclamation of "Hjckrrh!" by the Gryphon.

Between long pauses and much sobbing, the Mock Turtle tells a pun-filled tale. What follows is a satire of education: The titles of instructors and classes are mocked by puns, and the educational system is subject to absurdity. He states that he attended a school in the sea. The schoolmaster was an old turtle the students called Tortoise. The Gryphon and the Mock Turtle mock Alice when she asks the simple question of why the schoolmaster was called tortoise. It was not because he was an actual tortoise, but "because he taught us," answers the Mock Turtle, punning on the word "taught" in an accent that helps him pull it off.

Alice and the Gryphon sit and listen to the Mock Turtle's tale.
Mary Evans Picture Library

Continuing his story, the Mock Turtle says he went to school every day, and Alice replies that she, too, has been to day schools. The Mock Turtle wonders whether Alice's schooling offered "extras." Alice replied that she had lessons in French and music. Alice is putting on airs in an attempt to impress the Turtle. The Turtle's school offered those, too, she is informed, plus washing. Alice's middle-class tendencies cause her to be offended by the remark, inferring to the reader that she would find such menial tasks insulting. The Mock Turtle could not afford to take washing, however. He studied "reeling and writhing" and the different branches of Arithmetic—"Ambition, Distraction, Uglification, and Derision."

Alice questions him about the invented word "Uglification," but the Gryphon interrupts to ask if she knows the meaning of "beautify." When Alice shows that she knows the meaning of the term, the Gryphon exclaims that he expects then that she should know what "Uglification" means as well, and calls her a simpleton. Alice encourages the Mock Turtle to continue. The Mock Turtle notes that he also learned Mystery, Seaography, and Drawling. The Drawling class was taught by an old Conger-eel who instructed students on Drawling, Stretching, and Fainting in Coils.

The Mock Turtle and the Gryphon begin reminiscing sadly about their school days, and both hide their faces in their paws. Their excessive sentimentality makes them feel sad about everything, including their absurd schooling. Alice asks about the lesson schedules, and the Mock Turtle answers that students studied ten hours the first day, nine the next, and so on. The Gryphon informs her that the reduced schedule is why teachings are called lessons, "because they lessen from day to day."

Alice wonders whether the eleventh day, then, was a holiday. Of course, answers the Mock Turtle. Alice tries to find out about the twelfth day, but the Gryphon interrupts her to encourage the Mock Turtle to tell her something about the games played in school.

Chapter X: The Lobster Quadrille

The Gryphon and the Mock Turtle describe and dance the Lobster Quadrille, Alice tells them of her experiences that day, and she hears the Mock Turtle sob his way through the "Turtle Soup" song before leaving with the Gryphon to attend a trial.

The Mock Turtle sighed deeply, and drew the back of one flapper across his eyes. He looked at Alice, and tried to speak, but for a minute or two sobs choked his voice. "Same as if he had a bone in his throat," said the Gryphon: and it set to work shaking him and punching him in the back. At last the Mock Turtle recovered his voice, and, with tears running down his cheeks, he went on again:—

"You may not have lived much under the sea—" ("I haven't," said Alice)—"and perhaps you were never even introduced to a lobster—" (Alice began to say "I once tasted—" but checked herself hastily, and said "No, never") "—so you can have no idea what a delightful thing a Lobster **Quadrille** is!"

"No, indeed," said Alice. "What sort of a dance is it?"

"Why," said the Gryphon, "you first form into a line along the sea-shore—"

"Two lines!" cried the Mock Turtle. "Seals, turtles, salmon, and so on; then, when you've cleared all the jelly-fish out of the way—"

"*That* generally takes some time," interrupted the Gryphon.

"—you advance twice—"

"Each with a lobster as a partner!" cried the Gryphon.

"Of course," the Mock Turtle said: "advance twice, set to partners—"

"—change lobsters, and retire in same order," continued the Gryphon.

NOTES

→ more socially aware.

quadrille: a square dance of French origin, consisting of several figures, performed by four couples.

"Then, you know," the Mock Turtle went on, "you throw the—"

"The lobsters!" shouted the Gryphon, with a bound into the air.

"—as far out to sea as you can—"

"Swim after them!" screamed the Gryphon.

"Turn a somersault in the sea!" cried the Mock Turtle, capering wildly about.

"Change lobster's again!" yelled the Gryphon at the top of its voice.

"Back to land again, and that's all the first figure," said the Mock Turtle, suddenly dropping his voice; and the two creatures, who had been jumping about like mad things all this time, sat down again very sadly and quietly, and looked at Alice.

"It must be a very pretty dance," said Alice timidly.

"Would you like to see a little of it?" said the Mock Turtle.

"Very much indeed," said Alice.

"Come, let's try the first figure!" said the Mock Turtle to the Gryphon. "We can do without lobsters, you know. Which shall sing?"

"Oh, *you* sing," said the Gryphon. "I've forgotten the words."

So they began solemnly dancing round and round Alice, every now and then treading on her toes when they passed too close, and waving their forepaws to mark the time, while the Mock Turtle sang this, very slowly and sadly:—

*"Will you walk a little faster?" said a **whiting** to a snail.*
"There's a porpoise close behind us, and he's treading on my tail.
See how eagerly the lobsters and the turtles all advance!

whiting: any of various edible marine fishes.

They are waiting on the **shingle**—will you come
and join the dance?
        Will you, won't you, will you, won't you, will
you join the dance?
        Will you, won't you, will you, won't you,
won't you join the dance?
"You can really have no notion how delightful it
will be
When they take us up and throw us, with the lobsters, out to sea!"

violence.

But the snail replied "Too far, too far!" and gave a
look askance—
Said he thanked the whiting kindly, but he would
not join the dance.
        Would not, could not, would not, could not,
would not join the dance.
        Would not, could not, would not, could not,
could not join the dance.

parody of poem.

"What matters it how far we go?" his scaly friend
replied.
"There is another shore, you know, upon the other
side.
The further off from England the nearer is to
France—
Then turn not pale, beloved snail, but come and join
the dance.
        Will you, won't you, will you, won't you, will
you join the dance?
        Will you, won't you, will you, won't you,
won't you join the dance?"

"Thank you, it's a very interesting dance to
watch," said Alice, feeling very glad that it was
over at last: "and I do so like that curious song
about the whiting!"

is being polite.

"Oh, as to the whiting," said the Mock Turtle,
"they—you've seen them, of course?"

shingle: a large, coarse, waterworn gravel, as found on a beach.

"Yes," said Alice, "I've often seen them at dinn—" she checked herself hastily.

"I don't know where Dinn may be," said the Mock Turtle, "but if you've seen them so often, of course you know what they're like."

"I believe so," Alice replied thoughtfully. "They have their tails in their mouths—and they're all over crumbs."

"You're wrong about the crumbs," said the Mock Turtle: "crumbs would all wash off in the sea. But they *have* their tails in their mouths; and the reason is—" here the Mock Turtle yawned and shut his eyes.— "Tell her about the reason and all that," he said to the Gryphon.

"The reason is," said the Gryphon, "that they *would* go with the lobsters to the dance. So they got thrown out to sea. So they had to fall a long way. So they got their tails fast in their mouths. So they couldn't get them out again. That's all."

"Thank you," said Alice, "it's very interesting. I never knew so much about a whiting before."

"I can tell you more than that, if you like," said the Gryphon. "Do you know why it's called a whiting?"

"I never thought about it," said Alice. "Why?"

"*It does the boots and shoes*," the Gryphon replied very solemnly.

Alice was thoroughly puzzled. "Does the boots and shoes!" she repeated in a wondering tone.

"Why, what are *your* shoes done with?" said the Gryphon. "I mean, what makes them so shiny?" Alice looked down at them, and considered a little before she gave her answer. "They're done with blacking, I believe."

"Boots and shoes under the sea," the Gryphon went on in a deep voice, "are done with a whiting. Now you know."

"And what are they made of?" Alice asked in a tone of great curiosity.

"Soles and eels, of course," the Gryphon replied rather impatiently: "any shrimp could have told you that."

"If I'd been the whiting," said Alice, whose thoughts were still running on the song, "I'd have said to the porpoise, 'Keep back, please: we don't want *you* with us!'"

"They were obliged to have him with them," the Mock Turtle said: "no wise fish would go anywhere without a porpoise."

"Wouldn't it really?" said Alice in a tone of great surprise.

"Of course not," said the Mock Turtle: "why, if a fish came to *me*, and told me he was going a journey, I should say 'With what porpoise?'"

"Don't you mean 'purpose'?" said Alice.

"I mean what I say," the Mock Turtle replied in an offended tone. And the Gryphon added "Come, let's hear some of *your* adventures."

"I could tell you my adventures—beginning from this morning," said Alice a little timidly: "but it's no use going back to yesterday, because I was a different person then."

"Explain all that," said the Mock Turtle.

"No, no! The adventures first," said the Gryphon in an impatient tone: "explanations take such a dreadful time."

So Alice began telling them her adventures from the time when she first saw the White Rabbit. She was a little nervous about it just at first, the two creatures got so close to her, one on each side, and opened their eyes and mouths so *very* wide, but she gained courage as she went on. Her listeners were perfectly quiet till she got to the part about her repeating "*You are old, Father William,*" to the Caterpillar, and the words all coming different, and then the Mock Turtle drew a long breath, and said "That's very curious."

"It's all about as curious as it can be," said the Gryphon.

"It all came different!" the Mock Turtle repeated thoughtfully. "I should like to hear her try and repeat something now. Tell her to begin." He looked at the Gryphon as if he thought it had some kind of authority over Alice.

"Stand up and repeat ' *'Tis the voice of the **sluggard**,*'" said the Gryphon.

"How the creatures order one about, and make one repeat lessons!" thought Alice; "I might as well be at school at once." However, she got up, and began to repeat it, but her head was so full of the Lobster Quadrille, that she hardly knew what she was saying, and the words came very queer indeed:—

"'Tis the voice of the Lobster; I heard him declare,
'You have baked me too brown, I must sugar my
   hair.'
As a duck with its eyelids, so he with his nose
Trims his belt and his buttons, and turns out his toes.
When the sands are all dry, he is gay as a lark,
And will talk in contemptuous tones of the Shark,
But, when the tide rises and sharks are around,
His voice has a timid and tremulous sound."

"That's different from what I used to say when I was a child," said the Gryphon.

"Well, I never heard it before," said the Mock Turtle; "but it sounds uncommon nonsense." Alice said nothing; she had sat down with her face in her hands, wondering if anything would *ever* happen in a natural way again.

sluggard: a habitually lazy or idle person

"I should like to have it explained," said the Mock Turtle.

"She can't explain it," said the Gryphon hastily. "Go on with the next verse."

"But about his toes?" the Mock Turtle persisted. "How *could* he turn them out with his nose, you know?"

"It's the first position in dancing," Alice said; but was dreadfully puzzled by the whole thing, and longed to change the subject.

"Go on with the next verse," the Gryphon repeated impatiently: "it begins 'I passed by his garden.'"

Alice did not dare to disobey, though she felt sure it would all come wrong, and she went on in a trembling voice:—

"I passed by his garden, and marked, with one eye,
How the Owl and the Panther were sharing a pie—
The Panther took pie-crust, and gravy, and meat,
While the Owl had the dish as its share of the treat.
When the pie was all finished, the Owl, as a boon,
Was kindly permitted to pocket the spoon:
While the Panther received knife and fork with a
* growl,*
And concluded the banquet—"

"What *is* the use of repeating all that stuff," the Mock Turtle interrupted, "if you don't explain it as you go on? It's by far the most confusing thing I ever heard!"

"Yes, I think you'd better leave off," said the Gryphon: and Alice was only too glad to do so.

"Shall we try another figure of the Lobster Quadrille?" the Gryphon went on. "Or would you like the Mock Turtle to sing you a song?"

"Oh, a song, please, if the Mock Turtle would be
so kind," Alice replied, so eagerly that the
Gryphon said, in a rather offended tone, "Hm!
No accounting for tastes! Sing her 'Turtle Soup,'
will you, old fellow?"
The Mock Turtle sighed deeply, and began, in a
voice sometimes choked with sobs, to sing this:—

"Beautiful Soup, so rich and green,
Waiting in a hot tureen!
Who for such dainties would not stoop?
Soup of the evening, beautiful Soup!
Soup of the evening, beautiful Soup!
    Beau—ootiful Soo—oop!
    Beau—ootiful Soo—oop!
Soo—oop of the e—e—evening,
    Beautiful, beautiful Soup!

"Beautiful Soup! Who cares for fish,
Game, or any other dish?
Who would not give all else for two p
ennyworth only of beautiful Soup?
Pennyworth only of beautiful Soup?
    Beau—ootiful Soo—oop!
    Beau—ootiful Soo—oop!
Soo—oop of the e—e—evening,
    Beautiful, beauti—FUL SOUP!"

"Chorus again!" cried the Gryphon, and the Mock
Turtle had just begun to repeat it, when a cry of
"The trial's beginning!" was heard in the
distance.
"Come on!" cried the Gryphon, and, taking
Alice by the hand, it hurried off, without waiting
for the end of the song.
"What trial is it?" Alice panted as she ran; but
the Gryphon only answered "Come on!" and ran

the faster, while more and more faintly came, carried on the breeze that followed them, the melancholy words:—

"Soo—oop of the e—e—evening,
Beautiful, beautiful Soup!"

COMMENTARY

Chapter X focuses on Alice's continued conversation with the Mock Turtle and Gryphon. The short length of this chapter, focused as it is on more linguistic hijinks, along with the Lobster Quadrille dance and the Mock Turtle's song "Turtle Soup," leaves little room for interpretation. Nevertheless, major themes persist, including logic that results either in a sense of order or extreme chaos, and the parody of moralizing that implies only good can come from following rules.

Seemingly, Alice's prolonged encounter with the Turtle and Gryphon was actually intended as part of Chapter IX, which became two separate chapters to break up the length of Chapter IX and to bring the book's total chapter count to twelve. Alice's encounter with the Mock Turtle and the Gryphon is the only example in *Alice's Adventures in Wonderland* where a single episode is continued in another chapter.

As the chapter begins, the Mock Turtle continues his tale, but not before sighing deeply and sobbing. The Gryphon compares the Turtle's difficulty to having a bone lodged in one's throat, and he shakes and holds the Turtle to help him along. With tears running down his face, the Mock Turtle speaks of a dance called the Lobster Quadrille.

The Mock Turtle and the Gryphon take turns, sometimes interrupting each other, in describing

the dance. Dances called quadrilles are well structured, with the dancers moving in careful, pre-designed steps and motions. The execution of those movements results in an elegant harmony of motion. Similarly, the Lobster Quadrille begins with a careful structure, but like absurd statements made in Wonderland that are followed to logical and comic extremes, the Lobster Quadrille develops into preposterousness. The Mock Turtle and Gryphon explain that two lines are formed along the seashore by seals, turtles, salmon, and the like (but not jelly-fish: they are cleared out of the way—a time-consuming process, according to the Gryphon). Each participant has a lobster as a partner. At times, the dancers change lobsters, and at other times the lobsters are thrown out to sea. Dancers then swim out to the lobsters, perform somersaults in the sea, change lobsters again, and return to land. The Mock Turtle and the Gryphon are quite animated while describing the dance, but both sit down in sadness and silence when they conclude their descriptions.

Alice comments that the Lobster Quadrille must be a very pretty dance, and the Mock Turtle and the Gryphon offer to show her a little of it, without the lobsters. They begin dancing solemnly, while the Mock Turtle sings a slow and sad song. Although she lies to the Turtle and Gryphon that she believes the dance is very interesting to watch, Alice is glad when the long song and dance are over.

She inquires about a whiting (a type of fish) mentioned in the song, and the ensuing discussion of the whiting leads to several misinterpretations and puns. The misinterpretation arises when Alice proclaims her familiarity with whiting, but only in an edible sense—a familiarity that would be fearsome to the Turtle, who has a logical fear of being eaten. She catches herself before she reveals to the Turtle and Gryphon that she has eaten whiting in the past. But she continues to describe whitings as they look after they are prepared for eating: with their tails in their mouths and breaded. The Turtle corrects her about the breading, because he says the crumbs would wash off in the sea. He informs her, however, that she is correct that whitings have their tails in their mouths. He cannot explain why that is, however, and asks the Gryphon to explain. The Gryphon says the whitings tail-in-mouth phenomenon is caused by the fish accompanying the lobsters to the dance. When the fish are thrown with the lobsters out into the sea, their tails get planted firmly in their mouths during their fall and they are unable to remove them.

The Gryphon continues speaking, discussing the etymology of the word "whiting." Whiting, according to the Gryphon, has to do with boots and shoes. On land, when boots and shoes are shined, people call it "blacking," he explains. Under the sea, on the other hand, the process of shining boots and shoes is called whiting. The Gryphon goes on to explain that boots and shoes are made with soles and eels, the latter a Cockney pronunciation of "heels." Cockney is a regional London accent usually associated with working-class people with little education, an ironic twist for a character like the Gryphon so interested in schooling. The Gryphon's logic in discussing the etymology or origin of the word "whiting" is similar to others in Wonderland who assume that if Alice is knowledgeable about a subject then she should be familiar with the opposite of that subject.

Alice turns her attention to another line in the song ("'Will you walk a little faster?' said a whiting to a snail, / 'There's a porpoise close behind us, and he's treading on my tail'") to say that if she were the whiting, she would have told the porpoise to back off. The Mock Turtle replies that the whiting and the snail were obliged to have the porpoise because, "no wise fish would go anywhere without a porpoise." When Alice suggests that the Mock Turtle meant to say "purpose," he replies in an offended tone, "I mean what I say." Alice exhibits a degree of rudeness in correcting the Turtle's pun, and the Turtle responds with the Mad Hatter's dictum that he clearly spoke what he had originally intended to say.

The Gryphon encourages Alice to tell them of her adventures. She would have to begin such a story with this morning, she says, because she was a different person yesterday. The Mock Turtle asks her to explain her statement, but the Gryphon prefers to hear of her adventures first, because, "explanations take such a dreadful time." In this, the Gryphon seems to be a supporter of empiricism, wanting only to hear the details of Alice's adventures but no analysis of those adventures. Alice, meanwhile, indicates she is suffering an identity crisis because she is not the same person as she was earlier in the day.

The two creatures listen silently to Alice as she relates her tale from the time she first spied the White Rabbit to the moment she could not correctly recite "You are old, Father William" to the Caterpillar. The Mock Turtle considers her inability to remember the lines as very curious. He orders the Gryphon to ask Alice to repeat something. The Gryphon commands her to stand up and repeat "'Tis the voice of the sluggard" (a poem written by Isaac Watts pertaining to the sinfulness of sloth), an action that reminds Alice of being in school. During her recitation she mixes up the verse with images from the Lobster-Quadrille, and the words come out very queer. The Mock Turtle calls her version "uncommon nonsense." Alice, meanwhile, sits down with her face in her hands, wondering if anything is ever again going to happen in a natural way.

The Mock Turtle wants her to explain the verse, but again the Gryphon, who doesn't care for explanation but only wants her to recite another verse, usurps the Turtle's request for an explanation. Alice tries another verse, but the Mock Turtle interrupts, finding no use in repeating a verse if it is not explained. The Gryphon urges Alice to stop, and he offers either another round of the Lobster Quadrille or a song by the Mock Turtle. Alice opts for the song, which offends the Gryphon. The Gryphon remarks that Alice's lack of taste is on display, but, regardless, he asks the Mock Turtle to sing "Turtle Soup."

The Mock Turtle sings a song of praise for turtle soup, confronting, if sadly, his fear of death, of being eaten. He has just begun to repeat the chorus ("Beau—ootiful Soo—oop! / Beau—ootiful Soo—oop! / Soo—oop of the e—e—evening, / Beautiful, beautiful Soup!") at the urging of the Gryphon, when the three of them hear a cry from the distance: "The trial's beginning!" The Gryphon seizes Alice by the hand and leads her away. Alice tries to inquire about the trial, but the Gryphon runs faster and faster, while the Mock Turtle's chorus of "Turtle Soup" grows fainter.

Chapter XI: Who Stole the Tarts?

Alice attends the trial of the Knave of Hearts (who is accused of stealing tarts) where the White Rabbit serves as a Herald, the King of Hearts serves as judge and prosecutor, and a nervous Hatter provides poor testimony.

NOTES

The King and Queen of Hearts were seated on their throne when they arrived, with a great crowd assembled about them—all sorts of little birds and beasts, as well as the whole pack of cards: the Knave was standing before them, in chains, with a soldier on each side to guard him; and near the King was the White Rabbit, with a trumpet in one hand, and a scroll of parchment in the other. In the very middle of the court was a table, with a large dish of tarts upon it: they looked so good, that it made Alice quite hungry to look at them — "I wish they'd get the trial done," she thought, "and hand round the refreshments!" But there seemed to be no chance of this, so she began looking at everything about her, to pass away the time.

Alice had never been in a court of justice before, but she had read about them in books, and she was quite pleased to find that she knew the name of nearly everything there. "That's the judge," she said to herself, "because of his great wig." The judge, by the way, was the King; and as he wore his crown over the wig, (look at the frontispiece if you want to see how he did it,) he did not look at all comfortable, and it was certainly not becoming.

"And that's the **jury-box**," thought Alice, "and those twelve creatures," (she was obliged to say "creatures" you see, because some of them were animals, and some were birds), "I suppose they are the jurors." She said this last word two or three times over to herself, being rather proud of it: for she thought, and rightly too, that very few

jury-box: a place to seat a jury, which is a group of people sworn to hear the evidence and inquire into the facts in a law case, and to give a decision in accordance with their findings.

little girls of her age knew the meaning of it at all. However, "jury-men" would have done just as well.

The twelve jurors were all writing very busily on **slates.** "What are they doing?" Alice whispered to the Gryphon. "They can't have anything to put down yet, before the trial's begun."

"They're putting down their names," the Gryphon whispered in reply, "for fear they should forget them before the end of the trial."

"Stupid things!" Alice began in a loud, indignant voice, but she stopped hastily, for the White Rabbit cried out, "Silence in the court!" and the King put on his spectacles and looked anxiously round, to make out who was talking.

Alice could see, as well as if she were looking over their shoulders, that all the jurors were writing down "stupid things!" on their slates, and she could even make out that one of them didn't know how to spell "stupid," and that he had to ask his neighbour to tell him. "A nice muddle their slates'll be in before the trial's over!" thought Alice.

One of the jurors had a pencil that squeaked. This of course, Alice could not stand, and she went round the court and got behind him, and very soon found an opportunity of taking it away. She did it so quickly that the poor little juror (it was Bill, the Lizard) could not make out at all what had become of it; so, after hunting all about for it, he was obliged to write with one finger for the rest of the day; and this was of very little use, as it left no mark on the slate.

"Herald, read the accusation!" said the King. On this the White Rabbit blew three blasts on the trumpet, and then unrolled the parchment scroll, and read as follows:

slates: a thin tablet used for writing on.

The White Rabbit trumpets the court to order.
Mary Evans Picture Library

"The Queen of Hearts, she made some tarts,
    All on a summer day:
The Knave of Hearts, he stole those tarts,
    And took them quite away!"

"Consider your verdict," the King said to the jury.

"Not yet, not yet!" the Rabbit hastily interrupted. "There's a great deal to come before that!"

"Call the first witness," said the King; and the White Rabbit blew three blasts on the trumpet, and called out, "First witness!"

The first witness was the Hatter. He came in with a teacup in one hand and a piece of bread-and-butter in the other. "I beg pardon, your Majesty," he began, "for bringing these in: but I hadn't quite finished my tea when I was sent for."

"You ought to have finished," said the King. "When did you begin?"

The Hatter looked at the March Hare, who had followed him into the court, arm-in-arm with the Dormouse. "Fourteenth of March, I think it was," he said.

"Fifteenth," said the March Hare.

"Sixteenth," added the Dormouse.

"Write that down," the King said to the jury, and the jury eagerly wrote down all three dates on their slates, and then added them up, and reduced the answer to shillings and pence.

"Take off your hat," the King said to the Hatter.

"It isn't mine," said the Hatter.

"Stolen!" the King exclaimed, turning to the jury, who instantly made a memorandum of the fact.

"I keep them to sell," the Hatter added as an explanation; "I've none of my own. I'm a hatter."

Here the Queen put on her spectacles, and began
staring at the Hatter, who turned pale and
fidgeted.

"Give your evidence," said the King; "and don't
be nervous, or I'll have you executed on the
spot."

This did not seem to encourage the witness at
all: he kept shifting from one foot to the other,
looking uneasily at the Queen, and in his confusion he bit a large piece out of his teacup instead
of the bread-and-butter.

Just at this moment Alice felt a very curious sensation, which puzzled her a good deal until she
made out what it was: she was beginning to grow
larger again, and she thought at first she would
get up and leave the court; but on second
thoughts she decided to remain where she was as
long as there was room for her.

"I wish you wouldn't squeeze so," said the Dormouse, who was sitting next to her. "I can hardly
breathe."

"I can't help it," said Alice very meekly: "I'm
growing."

"You've no right to grow here," said the
Dormouse.

"Don't talk nonsense," said Alice more boldly:
"you know you're growing too."

"Yes, but I grow at a reasonable pace," said the
Dormouse: "not in that ridiculous fashion." And
he got up very sulkily and crossed over to the
other side of the court.

All this time the Queen had never left off staring
at the Hatter, and, just as the Dormouse crossed
the court, she said to one of the officers of the
court, "Bring me the list of the singers in the last
concert!" on which the wretched Hatter trembled so, that he shook both his shoes off.

The nervous Hatter nervously prepares to give his testimony.
Mary Evans Picture Library

"Give your evidence," the King repeated angrily, "or I'll have you executed, whether you're nervous or not."

"I'm a poor man, your Majesty," the Hatter began, in a trembling voice, "—and I hadn't begun my tea—not above a week or so—and what with the bread-and-butter getting so thin— and the twinkling of the tea—"

"The twinkling of the what?" said the King.

"It began with the tea," the Hatter replied.

"Of course twinkling begins with a T!" said the King sharply. "Do you take me for a dunce? Go on!"

"I'm a poor man," the Hatter went on, "and most things twinkled after that—only the March Hare said—"

"I didn't!" the March Hare interrupted in a great hurry.

"You did!" said the Hatter.

"I deny it!" said the March Hare.

"He denies it," said the King: "leave out that part."

"Well, at any rate, the Dormouse said—" the Hatter went on, looking anxiously round to see if he would deny it too: but the Dormouse denied nothing, being fast asleep.

"After that," continued the Hatter, "I cut some more bread-and-butter—"

"But what did the Dormouse say?" one of the jury asked.

"That I can't remember," said the Hatter.

"You *must* remember," remarked the King, "or I'll have you executed."

The miserable Hatter dropped his teacup and bread-and-butter, and went down on one knee. "I'm a poor man, your Majesty," he began.

"You're a very poor speaker," said the King.

Here one of the guinea-pigs cheered, and was

immediately suppressed by the officers of the court. (As that is rather a hard word, I will just explain to you how it was done. They had a large canvas bag, which tied up at the mouth with strings: into this they slipped the guinea-pig, head first, and then sat upon it.)

"I'm glad I've seen that done," thought Alice. "I've so often read in the newspapers, at the end of trials, 'There was some attempts at applause, which was immediately suppressed by the officers of the court,' and I never understood what it meant till now."

"If that's all you know about it, you may stand down," continued the King.

"I can't go no lower," said the Hatter: "I'm on the floor, as it is."

"Then you may *sit* down," the King replied.

Here the other guinea-pig cheered, and was suppressed.

"Come, that finished the guinea-pigs!" thought Alice. "Now we shall get on better."

"I'd rather finish my tea," said the Hatter, with an anxious look at the Queen, who was reading the list of singers.

"You may go," said the King, and the Hatter hurriedly left the court, without even waiting to put his shoes on.

"—and just take his head off outside," the Queen added to one of the officers: but the Hatter was out of sight before the officer could get to the door.

"Call the next witness!" said the King.

The next witness was the Duchess's cook. She carried the pepper-box in her hand, and Alice guessed who it was, even before she got into the court, by the way the people near the door began sneezing all at once.

"Give your evidence," said the King.

"Shan't," said the cook.

The King looked anxiously at the White Rabbit, who said in a low voice, "Your Majesty must cross-examine *this* witness."

"Well, if I must, I must," the King said, with a melancholy air, and, after folding his arms and frowning at the cook till his eyes were nearly out of sight, he said in a deep voice, "What are tarts made of?"

"Pepper, mostly," said the cook.

"Treacle," said a sleepy voice behind her.

"Collar that Dormouse," the Queen shrieked out. "Behead that Dormouse! Turn that Dormouse out of court! Suppress him! Pinch him! Off with his whiskers!"

For some minutes the whole court was in confusion, getting the Dormouse turned out, and, by the time they had settled down again, the cook had disappeared.

"Never mind!" said the King, with an air of great relief. "Call the next witness." And he added in an undertone to the Queen, "Really, my dear, *you* must cross-examine the next witness. It quite makes my forehead ache!"

Alice watched the White Rabbit as he fumbled over the list, feeling very curious to see what the next witness would be like, "—for they haven't got much evidence *yet*," she said to herself. Imagine her surprise, when the White Rabbit read out, at the top of his shrill little voice, the name "Alice!"

COMMENTARY

The final two chapters of the book cover the trial concerning who stole the Queen's tarts. The trial is seemingly as disorganized as the Caucus-race and about as effective. Chapter XI reintroduces the King and Queen of Hearts, the White Rabbit, the Duchess' cook, Bill the Lizard, and the participants of the Mad Tea Party. Although he escorts Alice to the trial and answers one of Alice's questions early on, the Gryphon disappears from the narrative. The trial as described by Carroll is a kangaroo court, which is to say that it is a broad parody of the legal system complete with powdered wigs and strained logic. The nightmarish qualities of the trial—wherein the King plays judge and executioner, the jury is ineffectual, and the witnesses consistently are badgered—is among the first courtroom lampoon, foreshadowing such twentieth-century literary classics as Franz Kafka's *The Trial*.

The Knave of Hearts stands accused of stealing the Queen's tarts.
Mary Evans Picture Library

The chapter begins when the Gryphon and Alice arrive at the trial. The King and Queen of Hearts are seated on their thrones, and the White Rabbit, holding a long scroll in one hand and a trumpet in the other, stands next to the King. Birds, beasts, and the whole deck of cards crowd into the courtroom. The Knave, guarded by two soldiers, stands in chains before the King and Queen. Almost all of the characters Alice has encountered in Wonderland are present at the trial. In the middle of the court is a table with a large dish of tarts on it.

Alice wants to eat some of the tarts, but because there seems no chance of any refreshments being served soon, she turns her attention to identifying things in the courtroom. The King is wearing a wig (with his crown on top), so he must be the judge, according to Alice. She identifies twelve creatures in a box as the jury. She refers to them as "creatures" because most of them are animals and some are birds. The members of the jury are each writing things on slates. Alice asks the Gryphon about what they're writing, because no evidence has yet been presented. The Gryphon informs her that the jurors are writing down their own names so they won't forget them before the end of the trial. Like Alice, it seems, they are not secure about their identities.

The King orders the Herald to read the accusation. The Herald proves to be the White Rabbit, who blows three blasts on his trumpet, and unrolls and reads from the scroll he is holding in the other hand: "The Queen of Hearts, she made some tarts, / All on a summer day: / The Knave of Hearts, he stole the tarts, / And took them quite away!"

After the accusation is read, the King asks the jury to consider their verdict. Once again, this time in a court of law, an authoritative figure attempts to reach a conclusion, in this case a verdict, before evidence of proof is offered. However, the Rabbit reminds him that there is much to do before then.

The King alerts the White Rabbit to call the first witness. The first witness is the Hatter. He apologizes for bringing a cup of tea and bread-and-butter with him, as he hasn't quite finished them. Of course, the reader remembers that, for the Hatter, it is always teatime due to his disagreement with Time. The King asks the Hatter when he began the meal, and the Hatter answers, "the fourteenth of March." The March Hare, who has accompanied the Hatter to court, corrects the date as the fifteenth, and the Dormouse, who sits next to Alice, adds "sixteenth." The King instructs the jurors to write down each date. The jurors add the dates together and convert the sum into a monetary amount. Carroll plays with relationships between logic and mathematics, as if "adding up" facts can automatically produce a logical result in the way that a mathematical problem can be solved.

The King orders the Hatter to remove his hat, but the Hatter replies that the hat isn't his. The hat is stolen, deduces the King, but the Hatter explains that he keeps hats to sell, but has none of his own. The Hatter turns pale and nervous when the Queen puts on her spectacles and stares at him. He grows so nervous that he inadvertently bites his teacup, instead of his bread. His nervousness is attributable to the fact that he wishes not to be recognized by the Queen, who already has ordered his execution.

Alice, meanwhile, begins to grow. With that growth comes a destruction of her stability. Throughout her experiences in Wonderland, Alice has experienced sudden changes in size that upset the natural growth and maturity process. Sitting in court, she is a child in an adult world. The Dormouse protests that her expanding size is beginning to crowd him and claims she has no right to grow in the courtroom. Alice replies that the Dormouse is also growing, but he reminds her that he is growing at a reasonable pace. The Dormouse leaves for the other side of the court. The King, meanwhile, orders the Hatter to provide his evidence or he will be executed.

The Hatter mentions that he is poor and then provides a confusing testimony, making a reference to a tea and engaging in a dialogue with the King where the word "tea," the letter "t," and other words beginning with a "t" are mixed up. He begins to quote the March Hare, but the Hare speaks up and denies the words even before the Hatter can quote him. Instead, the Hatter begins to quote the Dormouse, who is fast asleep, but the Hatter forgets what the Dormouse has said. After dropping his teacup, the Hatter bends to one knee and calls himself a poor man, to which the King replies sarcastically, "You're a *very* poor *speaker*," confusing the Hatter's use of "poor" (without wealth) with the adjective "poor," which connotes poorly executed. A guinea pig juror cheers the King's remark and has to be suppressed (a word the narrator describes by saying the guinea pig is slipped into a large canvas bag and sat on).

The King allows the Hatter to step down, but because the Hatter is already on the floor he states that he cannot step any lower. The King then allows the Hatter to leave. He manages to get outside the courtroom before the Queen adds, "and just take his head off outside."

The next witness is called. A great sneezing begins as the Duchess's cook enters the courtroom. The cook has nothing substantial to offer; yet she is asked to participate. Carroll suggests that such pointless formality is a means used by humans to contend with disorder. The cook refuses the King's order to give evidence. Pressed by the White Rabbit to cross-examine her, the King asks the cook to tell the court what tarts are made of. "Mostly pepper," she replies, and the Dormouse adds, "Treacle." A great confusion erupts as the Dormouse is suppressed. When order returns, the cook is gone. The King feels relieved at not having to confront the cook, whose refusal to answer a question compromised the rules and formality of the trial, and he requests that the Queen question the next witness.

As the White Rabbit fumbles over the list, Alice wonders who the next witness will be, observing that not much evidence has yet been presented. She is surprised when the White Rabbit calls out her name as the next witness.

Chapter XII: Alice's Evidence

Back to full size, Alice upends a jury, gives testimony to the King, stands up to the Queen, and is attacked by a deck of cards. She awakes at the riverbank, tells her sister her curious dream, and goes off to take tea.

NOTES

"Here!" cried Alice, quite forgetting in the flurry of the moment how large she had grown in the last few minutes, and she jumped up in such a hurry that she tipped over the jury-box with the edge of her skirt, upsetting all the jurymen on to the heads of the crowd below, and there they lay sprawling about, reminding her very much of a globe of goldfish she had accidentally upset the week before.

"Oh, I *beg* your pardon!" she exclaimed in a tone of great dismay, and began picking them up again as quickly as she could, for the accident of the goldfish kept running in her head, and she had a vague sort of idea that they must be collected at once and put back into the jury-box, or they would die.

"The trial cannot proceed," said the King in a very grave voice, "until all the jurymen are back in their proper places—*all*," he repeated with great emphasis, looking hard at Alice as he said so.

Alice looked at the jury-box, and saw that, in her haste, she had put the Lizard in head downwards, and the poor little thing was waving its tail about in a melancholy way, being quite unable to move. She soon got it out again, and put it right; "not that it signifies much," she said to herself; "I should think it would be *quite* as much use in the trial one way up as the other."

As soon as the jury had a little recovered from the shock of being upset, and their slates and pencils had been found and handed back to them, they set to work very diligently to write

out a history of the accident, all except the
Lizard, who seemed too much overcome to do
anything but sit with its mouth open, gazing up
into the roof of the court.

"What do you know about this business?" the
King said to Alice.

"Nothing," said Alice.

"Nothing *whatever*?" persisted the King.

"Nothing whatever," said Alice.

"That's very important," the King said, turning
to the jury. They were just beginning to write
this down on their slates, when the White Rabbit
interrupted: "*Un*important, your Majesty means,
of course," he said in a very respectful tone, but
frowning and making faces at him as he spoke.

"*Un*important, of course, I meant," the King
hastily said, and went on to himself in an undertone, "important—unimportant—unimportant—important—" as if he were trying which
word sounded best.

Some of the jury wrote it down "important,"
and some "unimportant." Alice could see this, as
she was near enough to look over their slates;
"but it doesn't matter a bit," she thought to
herself.

At this moment the King, who had been for
some time busily writing in his note-book, cack-
led out "Silence!" and read out from his book,
"Rule Forty-two. *All persons more than a mile
high to leave the court.*"

Everybody looked at Alice.

"*I'm* not a mile high," said Alice.

"You are," said the King.

"Nearly two miles high," added the Queen.

"Well, I shan't go, at any rate," said Alice:
"besides, that's not a regular rule: you invented it
just now."

"It's the oldest rule in the book," said the King.

"Then it ought to be Number One," said Alice. The King turned pale, and shut his note-book hastily. "Consider your verdict," he said to the jury, in a low, trembling voice.

"There's more evidence to come yet, please your Majesty," said the White Rabbit, jumping up in a great hurry; "this paper has just been picked up."

"What's in it?" said the Queen.

"I haven't opened it yet," said the White Rabbit, "but it seems to be a letter, written by the prisoner to—to somebody."

"It must have been that," said the King, "unless it was written to nobody, which isn't usual, you know."

"Who is it directed to?" said one of the jurymen.

"It isn't directed at all," said the White Rabbit; "in fact, there's nothing written on the *outside*." He unfolded the paper as he spoke, and added "It isn't a letter, after all: it's a set of verses."

"Are they in the prisoner's handwriting?" asked another of they jurymen.

"No, they're not," said the White Rabbit, "and that's the queerest thing about it." (The jury all looked puzzled.)

"He must have imitated somebody else's hand," said the King. (The jury all brightened up again.)

"Please your Majesty," said the Knave, "I didn't write it, and they can't prove I did: there's no name signed at the end."

"If you didn't sign it," said the King, "that only makes the matter worse. You *must* have meant some mischief, or else you'd have signed your name like an honest man."

There was a general clapping of hands at this: it was the first really clever thing the King had said that day.

"That *proves* his guilt," said the Queen.

"It proves nothing of the sort!" said Alice. "Why, you don't even know what they're about!"

"Read them," said the King.

The White Rabbit put on his spectacles. "Where shall I begin, please your Majesty?" he asked.

"Begin at the beginning," the King said gravely, "and go on till you come to the end: then stop."

These were the verses the White Rabbit read:

> *"They told me you had been to her,*
>   *And mentioned me to him:*
> *She gave me a good character,*
>   *But said I could not swim.*
>
> *He sent them word I had not gone*
>   *(We know it to be true):*
> *If she should push the matter on,*
>   *What would become of you?*
>
> *I gave her one, they gave him two,*
>   *You gave us three or more;*
> *They all returned from him to you,*
>   *Though they were mine before.*
>
> *If I or she should chance to be*
>   *Involved in this affair,*
> *He trusts to you to set them free,*
>   *Exactly as we were.*
>
> *My notion was that you had been*
>   *(Before she had this **fit**)*
> *An obstacle that came between*
>   *Him, and ourselves, and it.*
>
> *Don't let him know she liked them best,*
>   *For this must ever be*
> *A secret, kept from all the rest,*
>   *Between yourself and me."*

fit: a sharp, brief display of feeling as in a "fit of anger."

"That's the most important piece of evidence we've heard yet," said the King, rubbing his hands; "so now let the jury—"

"If any one of them can explain it," said Alice, (she had grown so large in the last few minutes that she wasn't a bit afraid of interrupting him,) "I'll give him **sixpence**. *I* don't believe there's an atom of meaning in it."

The jury all wrote down on their slates, "*She* doesn't believe there's an atom of meaning in it," but none of them attempted to explain the paper.

"If there's no meaning in it," said the King, "that saves a world of trouble, you know, as we needn't try to find any. And yet I don't know," he went on, spreading out the verses on his knee, and looking at them with one eye; "I seem to see some meaning in them, after all. '—*said I could not swim*—' you can't swim, can you?" he added, turning to the Knave.

The Knave shook his head sadly. "Do I look like it?" he said. (Which he certainly did *not*, being made entirely of cardboard.)

"All right, so far," said the King, and he went on muttering over the verses to himself: "'*We know it to be true*—' that's the jury, of course—'*I gave her one, they gave him two*—' why, that must be what he did with the tarts, you know—"

"But, it goes on '*They all returned from him to you*,'" said Alice.

"Why, there they are!" said the King triumphantly, pointing to the tarts on the table. "Nothing can be clearer than *that*. Then again— '*Before she had this fit*—' you never had fits, my dear, I think?" he said to the Queen.

"Never!" said the Queen furiously, throwing an inkstand at the Lizard as she spoke. (The unfortunate little Bill had left off writing on his

sixpence: a former British coin equal in value to six pennies.

slate with one finger, as he found it made no
mark; but he now hastily began again, using the
ink, that was trickling down his face, as long as it
lasted.)

"Then the words don't *fit* you," said the King,
looking round the court with a smile. There was
a dead silence.

"It's a pun!" the King added in an offended tone,
and everybody laughed. "Let the jury consider
their verdict," the King said, for about the twentieth time that day.

"No, no!" said the Queen. "Sentence first—
verdict afterwards."

"Stuff and nonsense!" said Alice loudly. "The
idea of having the sentence first!"

"Hold your tongue!" said the Queen, turning
purple.

"I won't!" said Alice.

"Off with her head!" the Queen shouted at the
top of her voice. Nobody moved.

"Who cares for you?" said Alice, (she had grown
to her full size by this time.) "You're nothing but
a pack of cards!"

At this the whole pack rose up into the air, and
came flying down upon her: she gave a little
scream, half of fright and half of anger, and tried
to beat them off, and found herself lying on the
bank, with her head in the lap of her sister, who
was gently brushing away some dead leaves that
had fluttered down from the trees upon her face.

"Wake up, Alice dear!" said her sister; "Why,
what a long sleep you've had!"

"Oh, I've had such a curious dream!" said Alice,
and she told her sister, as well as she could
remember them, all these strange Adventures of
hers that you have just been reading about; and
when she had finished, her sister kissed her, and
said, "It *was* a curious dream, dear, certainly: but

now run in to your tea; it's getting late." So Alice got up and ran off, thinking while she ran, as well she might, what a wonderful dream it had been.

But her sister sat still just as she left her, leaning her head on her hand, watching the setting sun, and thinking of little Alice and all her wonderful Adventures, till she too began dreaming after a fashion, and this was her dream:—

First, she dreamed of little Alice herself, and once again the tiny hands were clasped upon her knee, and the bright eager eyes were looking up into hers—she could hear the very tones of her voice, and see that queer little toss of her head to keep back the wandering hair that *would* always get into her eyes—and still as she listened, or seemed to listen, the whole place around her became alive the strange creatures of her little sister's dream.

The long grass rustled at her feet as the White Rabbit hurried by—the frightened Mouse splashed his way through the neighbouring pool—she could hear the rattle of the teacups as the March Hare and his friends shared their never-ending meal, and the shrill voice of the Queen ordering off her unfortunate guests to execution—once more the pig-baby was sneezing on the Duchess's knee, while plates and dishes crashed around it—once more the shriek of the Gryphon, the squeaking of the Lizard's slate-pencil, and the choking of the suppressed guinea-pigs, filled the air, mixed up with the distant sobs of the miserable Mock Turtle.

So she sat on, with closed eyes, and half believed herself in Wonderland, though she knew she had but to open them again, and all would change to dull reality—the grass would be only rustling in the wind, and the pool rippling to the waving of

the reeds—the rattling teacups would change to
tinkling sheep-bells, and the Queen's shrill cries
to the voice of the shepherd boy—and the sneeze
of the baby, the shriek of the Gryphon, and all
the other queer noises, would change (she knew)
to the confused clamour of the busy farm-yard—
while the lowing of the cattle in the distance
would take the place of the Mock Turtle's heavy
sobs.

Lastly, she pictured to herself how this same little
sister of hers would, in the after-time, be herself
a grown woman; and how she would keep,
through all her riper years, the simple and loving
heart of her childhood: and how she would
gather about her other little children, and make
their eyes bright and eager with many a strange
tale, perhaps even with the dream of Wonderland of long ago: and how she would feel with all
their simple sorrows, and find a pleasure in all
their simple joys, remembering her own child-
life, and the happy summer days.

THE END

COMMENTARY

The final chapter of *Alice's Adventures in Wonderland* continues the trial of the Knave of Hearts, which concludes in pandemonium. As the chapter progresses, the fact that Alice is an active participant in her own dream becomes increasingly clear.

When the chapter begins, Alice jumps up upon hearing her name called. She forgets that she has grown larger, and her sudden movement tips over the jury box, scattering the jurors among the rest of the gathering. Alice has suddenly become a threat of annihilation. It reminds her of the time, just a week earlier, when she tipped over a goldfish bowl in her parents' home. This, perhaps, is Carroll's attempt to provide a psychological clue as to the frenzied, often violent, and stressful nature of Alice's dream of Wonderland. She begins picking up jurors and apologizing; in her mind, she remembers that she had to pick up the goldfish quickly after she spilled the bowl, or they would die. The line of demarcation between Alice's dream and her reality is continuing to blur.

The King says in a very grave voice while looking at Alice that the trial cannot proceed until all the jurors are in their proper places. Alice looks over to the jury box and realizes that she has placed Bill the Lizard upside down. As Alice picks up Bill and replaces him in an upright position, she considers that her action will have no bearing upon the outcome of the trial. The jurors, meanwhile, find their slates and pencils and proceed to write about what has just occurred. The jurors persist in following formality amid the topsy-turvy events: They are jurors, and, as such, they are supposed to take notes.

The King asks Alice what she knows of the stealing of the tarts, and Alice replies that she knows nothing of it. The King emphasizes to the jury that her remark is important, but the White Rabbit interrupts him to inform the King that Alice's remark is *un*important. The King agrees, then alternately says "important" and "unimportant," and some of the jurors write "important" on their slates, while others write "unimportant." In this instance, the King clearly doesn't say what he means, because he doesn't know what he means. What is considered important or unimportant is arbitrary in a trial where insignificant details are stressed and important points overlooked.

Normal processes are subverted in this court of law where mayhem is constant and the threat of death looms. In Carroll's satiric approach, courts and laws seem to be on trial. The King is the ultimate authority and representative of this esteemed court of law in Wonderland, but we find that his judgments are based not on law but on personal preference.

The King writes something down in a notebook, and then reads aloud Rule Forty-two from the notebook: "All persons more than a mile high to leave the courtroom." Everyone looks at Alice, but she remarks that she is not a mile high. The King disagrees, and the Queen states that Alice is nearly two-miles high.

Alice refuses to leave, noting that the rule has just been invented. The King counters that it is the oldest rule in the book, to which Alice replies, "Then it ought to be Number One." The King turns pale at being logically out-maneuvered by Alice, and orders the jury to consider their verdict. The White Rabbit interrupts to say that more evidence needs to be presented, and he notes a piece of paper that has just been discovered. The Queen demands to know its contents, and the White Rabbit replies that it is a letter written by the prisoner to somebody.

The letter isn't directed to anyone, the Rabbit informs the gathering, because no one's name appears on the outside. After he unfolds the letter, he announces that it contains a set of verses. The verses are not written in the prisoner's handwriting, he declares. The King concludes that the prisoner has imitated someone else's handwriting. Using logic based on a questionable supposition, the King assumes that the Knave is guilty by omitting his signature, as he would prove his honesty if he did indeed sign the verses. The King concludes, then, that the Knave is dishonest and he has forged someone else's handwriting.

The King's supposition moves to a humorously logical conclusion. The prisoner disclaims the King's finding, saying that because there was no name signed at the end of the letter, proving that he wrote it is impossible. The King replies that lack of a signature only makes the matter worse: The prisoner would have signed it unless he had been up to some mischief, according to the King. "That *proves* his guilt," reasons the Queen, and she is in the process of saying "off with his head" when Alice interrupts her. Alice correctly claims that the court has proven nothing, and that no one yet knows what the verse is about. It is interesting to note that as Alice grows in physical stature, her maturity and confidence grow as well.

The Rabbit dons spectacles and asks the King where to begin reading. Gravely, the King responds that he should begin at the beginning and end at the end. Read aloud, the verse seems nonsensical, but the King calls it the most important piece of evidence yet. Emboldened because she has grown so large, Alice disagrees with the King. She states that she doesn't believe that the letter holds "an atom of meaning." In this, she is incorrect. She assumes that the verses are written objectively and that the pronouns in the poem do not relate to

actual individuals. The jurors write down her statement, but they do not attempt to interpret the verse. In a situation where some misinterpret and others do not attempt to interpret, how can any real meaning exist, Carroll seems to imply.

The King, meanwhile, notes that if the letter has no meaning, then no one needs to try to find any. Still, he pursues an interpretation. Taking a line that states "I could not swim," he asks the prisoner, the Knave of Hearts, whether or not he can swim (he can't, being made of cardboard). The King then makes casual associations with the Knave and the rest of the lines.

He stumbles on the line, "Before she had this fit," which seems directed at the Queen, well known for her fits of displeasure. To the question of whether she ever has fits, the Queen shouts "Never!" while throwing an inkstand at one of the jurors. The unlucky juror hit by the object is Bill the Lizard.

"Then the words don't *fit* you," the King says to the Queen, but no one understands his pun. He angrily points out the pun, and then everyone laughs. The arbitrariness of power is exposed by the fact that the King can make people laugh, if not by his comedic talent, then by his vested authority.

The King again calls for the jury to consider its verdict, but the Queen intervenes: "Sentence first—verdict afterwards," she cries. Alice calls the idea of having a sentence precede a verdict nonsense, setting up a struggle between she and the Queen. The Queen orders her to hold her tongue; when Alice refuses, the Queen shouts "Off with her head!" In the adult world represented by the Queen, illogic can become logic when backed with authority. Alice manages this adult absurdity when she cries, "nonsense!" She has learned to

Alice fights off a pack of angry cards before waking and realizing that her adventure in Wonderland was a dream.
Mary Evans Picture Library

Alice tells her sister that she has had a curious dream, and she relates the things that happened—all the strange events. Her sister kisses her when Alice finishes her story, and she tells Alice to rush home, for it is teatime. A sense of normalcy returns. As Alice runs home, her sister remains at the riverbank, watching the sunset and thinking of Alice's dream until she too begins dreaming. She dreams of Alice—her small hands, the way she lightly tosses her head to keep the hair from her eyes, the tone of her voice, and all the strange creatures she described. Elements of fantasy and dream are connected with objects and events in the real world, as Alice's sister projects her own sense of logic on the world. That logic, in the end, is tinged with sentimentality.

Alice's sister half-believes that she is in Wonderland. She knows, however, that when she opens her eyes the rattling of teacups will prove to be a sheep bell and that all the other odd noises of a barnyard have been transformed into sounds of the creatures in Wonderland.

Alice's sister then pictures the future—when Alice is a grown woman but retains the heart of her childhood years. She pictures Alice telling strange tales to her children and the children of other people, and that they, too, will dream of Wonderland. Alice, then, will feel their pleasures and sorrows and recall the happy summer days of her own childhood. Simple joys are valued over maturity in this outlook, and Wonderland is considered stimulating, but never as satisfying as the pleasures and sorrows of childhood experience.

rely on her own perceptions of reality and can challenge and overcome that which threatens her. Struggling against adult authority and restraint, she denies a terrifying reality of being beheaded.

Alice has grown full size by this time. Challenging the Queen's pronouncement, she says to her and many in the gathering, "You're nothing but a pack of cards!" The whole pack of cards suddenly fly at her, and she begins fighting them off when she becomes aware that she is lying on a riverbank in the lap of her sister, who is gently brushing away leaves from Alice's hair. She tells Alice to wake up.

CLIFFSCOMPLETE REVIEW

Use this CliffsComplete Review to gauge what you've learned and to build confidence in your understanding of the original text. After you work through the review questions, the problem-solving exercises, and the suggested activities, you're well on your way to understanding and appreciating *Alice's Adventures in Wonderland.*

Identify the Quotation

Identify the following quotations by answering these questions:

* Who is the speaker of the quote?

* What does it reveal about the speaker's character?

* What does it tell us about other characters within the novel?

* Where does it occur within the novel?

* What does it show us about the themes of the novel?

* What significant imagery do you see in the quote, and how do these images relate to the overall imagery of the novel?

1. Boots and shoes under the sea are done with whiting. Now you know.

2. Well, then, you see a dog growls when it's angry, and wags its tail when it's pleased. Now I growl when I'm pleased, and wag my tail when I'm angry. Therefore I'm mad.

3. Speak roughly to your little boy,
   And beat him when he sneezes:
   He only does it to annoy,
   Because he knows it teases.

4. One side will make you grow taller, and the other side will make you grow shorter.

5. And yet what a dear little puppy it was! I should have liked teaching it tricks very much, if—if I'd only been the right size to do it!

6. *Everybody* has won and *all* must have prizes.

7. Why, there they are! Nothing can be clearer that *that*. Then again—'*before she had this fit*'—you never had *fits*, my dear I think?

8. Collar that Dormouse. Behead that Dormouse! Turn that Dormouse out of court! Suppress him! Pinch him! Off with his whiskers!

9. Reeling and Writing, of course, to begin with, and then the different branches of Arithmetic—Ambition, Distraction, Uglification, and Derision.

10. Ah! That accounts for it. He won't stand beating. Now, if you only kept on good terms with him, he'd do almost anything you liked with the clock. For instance, suppose it were nine o'clock in the morning, just time to begin lessons; you'd only have to whisper a hint to Time, and round goes the clock in a twinkling! Half-past one, time for dinner!

True/False

1. T F Alice makes many friends in Wonderland.

2. T F Dinah is Alice's pet cat.

3. T F The Lobster Quadraille is a military exercise.

4. T F The Mock Turtle is actually a Tortoise.

5. T F The White Rabbit tells a long tale.

6. T F The Mad Hatter was once good friends with Time.

7. T F The Caterpillar introduces Alice to the Duchess.

8. T F All Cheshire cats smile.

9. T F One of the footman in livery is really a frog.

10. T F In the Queen's croquet game, the mallets are flamingos and the balls are hamsters.

11. T F The Duchess's baby turns into a baby pig.

12. T F Alice falls into a pool of her own tears.

13. T F The Knave of Hearts is found guilty of stealing the tarts.

14. T F The Queen of Hearts is fond of finding morals.

15. T F The March Hare and Mad Hatter push the Dormouse into a treacle well.

Multiple Choice

1. The book's finale contains the thoughts of whom?
   a. Dinah
   b. Alice
   c. Alice's sister
   d. The White Rabbit

2. From who does Alice learn the Lobster Quadrille?
   a. The March Hare and the Mad Hatter
   b. The Duchess and the cook
   c. The Gryphon and the Mock Turtle
   d. Pat and Bill the Lizard

3. Who sends Alice to hear the Mock Turtle's history?
   a. The Queen
   b. The Duchess
   c. The Gryphon
   d. The Cheshire Cat

4. What is the name of the White Rabbit's housemaid?
   a. Dinah
   b. Elsie
   c. Eleanor
   d. Mary Ann

5. Who is among those competing in the Caucus-race?
   a. The White Rabbit and Bill the Lizard
   b. The Dodo and the Eaglet
   c. The Dormouse and the March Hare
   d. The Queen of Hearts and the Duchess

6. Alice nearly drowns in a pool of water formed by what?

   a. Her own tears

   b. Spilled tea

   c. Water from a hookah

   d. Rain

7. When Alice falls down the rabbit hole, where does she eventually land?

   a. On a pile of sticks and leaves

   b. On the White Rabbit

   c. In a pool of water

   d. On a giant mushroom

8. What does the label on the bottle that Alice finds in the long, low hall say?

   a. Drink me

   b. Poison

   c. Save for later

   d. No deposit, no return

9. As Alice changes size in Chapter II, what does she notice she's wearing?

   a. The White Rabbit's pocket watch

   b. The White Rabbit's waistcoat

   c. The White Rabbit's kid glove

   d. The White Rabbit's whiskers

10. For what is Pat digging when he is introduced?

   a. Bananas

   b. Apples

   c. Rutabegas

   d. Celery

11. What do the stones thrown at Alice while she's trapped in the White Rabbit's house turn into?

   a. Mushrooms

   b. Lizards

   c. Cakes

   d. Tarts

12. What is the Caterpillar's height?

   a. Exactly three-inches tall

   b. Seventeen-and-a-half-inches tall

   c. Exactly twelve-inches tall

   d. Approximately one-and-a-half-inches tall

13. For what does the Pigeon mistake Alice?

   a. A lizard

   b. Another pigeon

   c. A serpent

   d. The Queen of Hearts

14. How does Alice enter the Duchess's house?

   a. By waiting for the footman to open the door

   b. By letting herself in

   c. By knocking very loudly

   d. By following the Cheshire Cat

15. How does Alice identify the March Hare's house?

   a. By a sign posted on the house's door

   b. By its ear-shaped chimneys and fur-thatched roof

   c. By the scent of fresh tea and cakes

   d. By the loud clamor coming from inside

Fill in the Blank

1. Instead of Latin and Greek, the Gryphon's Classical Master taught _____ and _____.

2. When questioned what tarts are made of, the cook responds that they are mostly made of _____.

3. In the Dormouse's story, the three sisters draw items that begin with the letter _____.

4. The Pigeon reasons that Alice is a serpent because she eats _____.

5. Father William is able to eat a goose's bones and beak because practicing _____ strengthened his jaw.

6. Bill the Lizard enters the White Rabbit's house by climbing in the _____.

7. Alice frightens the Mouse and the Lory, the Dodo, and the other birds by bragging about her _____.

8. According to the Gryphon, the opposite of beautification is _____.

9. The Knave of Hearts is completely made of _____.

10. The Queen demands that the court "Sentence first _____."

Discussion

Use the following questions to generate discussion:

1. *Alice's Adventures in Wonderland* contains many violent images and threatening actions. How does the references to violence add or detract from the novel's classification as a children's work?

2. Many critics perceive *Alice's Adventures in Wonderland* as a work of satire. What or who is/are being satirized?

3. What was Carroll's attitude or opinion toward several of the many examples of irrationality, illogic, and fallacious reasoning in *Alice's Adventures in Wonderland*?

4. Much of *Alice's Adventures in Wonderland* is concerned with misunderstandings based on misinterpretations of the meanings of certain words and phrases. What do you think Carroll is saying about the nature of spoken communication?

5. Many people think that because the Caterpillar smokes a hookah and encourages Alice to partake of the mushroom, Carroll himself used drugs. Do you agree or disagree? Why or why not?

6. Some critics believe that Carroll's interest in young females was of an improper sexual nature. Can you find any evidence in *Alice's Adventures in Wonderland* to support or refute this claim?

7. Carroll makes several references to children's education in *Alice's Adventures in Wonderland*. Do you think he is attempting to make a serious point? Why or why not?

8. Discuss the ending of the story. Is there any other way Carroll could have ended it? Why or why not?

9. What do you believe Carroll's true intention was in writing *Alice's Adventures in Wonderland*? Do you believe he was successful?

10. Can *Alice's Adventures in Wonderland* truly be called a children's book? Or does it work as successfully as a book for adults to read as well? Explain your answer.

Identifying Fiction Elements

Find examples of the following elements in the text of *Alice's Adventures in Wonderland*:

* **Puns** (a word or phrase used with two or more meanings)

* **Parody** (a literary or musical work imitating the style of another work)

* **Malapropisms** (a ludicrous misuse of words caused by a resemblance in sound)

* **Homonyms** (a word with the same pronunciation as another but with a different meaning, origin, and, usual spelling)

* **Anthropomorphism** (the attributing of human shape or characteristics to a god, animal, or inanimate thing)

* **Similes** (a figure of speech in which one thing is likened to another, dissimilar thing by the use of like, as, etc.)

* **Metaphors** (a figure of speech containing an implied comparison, in which a word or phrase ordinarily and primarily used of one thing is applied to another)

* **Hyperbole** (exaggeration for effect and not meant to be taken literally)

* **Oxymoron** (a figure of speech in which opposite or contradictory ideas or terms are combined)

* **Onomatopoeia** (formation of a word by imitating the natural sound associated with the object or action involved)

Activities

The following activities can springboard you into further discussions and projects:

1. Make a list of your favorite characters (those you positively identify with the most) and least favorite characters in the book. Rank the characters. Explain what it is about the character that you admire or don't admire.

2. Read *Through the Looking-Glass: And What Alice Found There,* the sequel to *Alice's Adventures in Wonderland,* and report to your classmates how the two books handle the same themes. Does the sequel "measure up" to the original work? How are they alike? How are they dissimilar?

3. View several film adaptations of *Alice's Adventures in Wonderland.* Set up a panel discussion in class, in which you play movie critics. Discuss whether the film versions live up to your expectations. What is gained by turning *Alice's Adventures in Wonderland* into a movie? What is lost? Is too much time spent on material from *Through the Looking-Glass: And What Alice Found There?* Do certain characters differ greatly in the film versions when compared to their depictions in the book?

4. Much of *Alice's Adventures in Wonderland* concerns the nature of language. In fact, several noted philosophers have used Carroll's work to underscore their belief that language is inherently incapable of conveying exactly what the speaker means to say. Using examples from *Alice's Adventures in Wonderland,* agree or disagree that language is a flawed system of communication.

5. Write your own adventure for Alice in which you introduce her to a new character that you have invented. This character may present a new theme such as the unreliability of perceptions, class differences, social attitudes, or economics.

6. Rewrite the final scene as a first-person narrative. Imagine you are Alice's sister and are thinking the thoughts represented by Carroll in the original work.

7. Select and act out one scene with several of your classmates. Try to portray what each character might actually represent according to what you know about Carroll. Now, imagine that your characters are outside the scene you selected. While remaining in character, show how the characters would react to hearing modern slang expressions, advertising slogans, and lyrics from popular music.

8. Keep a journal in which you write down how modern-day life resembles episodes from *Alice's Adventures in Wonderland*. Also note how many times actual references are made to the characters and illogic of Wonderland.

9. In film versions of *Alice's Adventures in Wonderland*, Alice is alternately depicted as a demure, polite little girl and as a precocious, outspoken and ill-mannered child. Using examples from Carroll's book and the film adaptations you have viewed, compare and contrast these depictions and discuss which is the most accurate according to Carroll's original descriptions of her.

10. Stage a mock trial in which each character is accused of a different crime. For example, the Mock Turtle can be accused of impersonating a real turtle, and Alice can be accused of truancy. Make sure that each character is acted in accordance with their respective depictions in the book.

Answers

Identify the Quotation

1. From Chapter X, the Gryphon explains that, if boots are shined by blackening on land, they are shined using whiting (a pun on the type of fish) in the sea.

2. From Chapter VI, the Cheshire Cat explains that he is mad by presenting a negative comparison with a dog.

3. From Chapter VI, the Duchess sings to her little baby who'll soon enough transform into a pig.

4. From Chapter V, the Caterpillar instructs Alice how to eat the mushroom that will either make her bigger or smaller.

5. From Chapter IV, Alice reflects on her encounter with a full-size puppy while she was only several inches tall.

6. From Chapter III, the Dodo declares that the Caucus-race, which had no rules, must declare all competitors a winner.

7. From Chapter XII, the King reads the nonsense verse attributed to the Knave at his trial.

8. From Chapter XI, the Queen threatens the Dormouse for uttering "treacle" in the courtroom.

9. From Chapter IX, the Mock Turtle describes for Alice the regular course in the school he attended.

10. From Chapter VII, the Mad Hatter discusses the personification of Time with Alice.

True/False

1. F 2. T 3. F 4. F 5. F 6. T 7. F 8. T 9. T 10. F 11. T 12. T 13. F 14. F 15. F

Multiple Choice

1. c 2. c 3. a 4. d 5. b 6. a 7. a 8. a 9. c 10. b 11. c 12. a 13. c 14. b 15. b

Fill in the Blank

1. Laughing and Grief 2. pepper 3. M 4. eggs 5. law 6. chimney 7. cat, Dinah 8. Uglification 9. cardboard 10. verdict afterwards

CLIFFSCOMPLETE RESOURCE CENTER

The learning doesn't need to stop here. CliffsComplete Resource Center shows you the best of the best: great links to information in print, on film, and online. And the following aren't all the great resources available to you; visit www.cliffsnotes.com for tips on reading literature, writing papers, giving presentations, locating other resources, and testing your knowledge.

Books, Magazines, and Articles

Auerbach, Nina. "Alice and Wonderland: A Curious Child." *Victorian Studies*, Vol. XVIII, No. 1 (September 1973): 31-47.

Auerbach considers Alice to embody the various qualities of Victorian England childhood. Auerbach also addresses many of the psychoanalytic analyses of Carroll's work.

Beerbohm, Max. "Alice Again Awakened." *Around Theatres, Vol. I.* Alfred A. Knopf. 1939.

Beerbohm's article, originally published in *The Saturday Review*, puts forth his belief that Alice's adventures are morality tales; that she has been naughty and is working out her redemption through her encounters with the Caterpillar, Queen, and other characters.

Chesterton, G. K. "Lewis Carroll." *A Handful of Authors: Essays on Books & Writers.* Sheed and Ward. 1953.

Chesterton's classic essay humorously exhibits his fear that Carroll's works will become established classics. Such a fate, Chesterton writes, will render the books stuffy and academic, depleting them of their fantastical and fun quotient.

Cohen, Morton N., editor. *The Letters of Lewis Carroll.* Oxford University Press, 1979.

These two volumes collect most of Carroll's letters, which are notable for the entertainingly and engagingly familiar manner of Carroll's output.

Collingwood, Stuart Dodgson. *The Life and Letters of Lewis Carroll.* 1898.

This is the first biography of Carroll, which was written by his nephew. It remains unsurpassed for its rendering of the facts of Carroll's life.

De la Mare, Walter. *Lewis Carroll.* Faber and Faber Ltd. 1932.

De la Mare is highly complimentary of Carroll's *Alice* books, finding them to be works of genius and lauding the works' ingenious internal structures.

Empson, William. "Alice in Wonderland." *Some Versions of Pastoral.* Chatto & Windus, 1935.

Empson's article famously argues that Alice embodies all human sexual qualities; her entering the Rabbit's hole is a masculine penetration, she is in utero when she lands on the pile of sticks, and she must find her femininity in order to remove herself from Wonderland.

Flescher, Jacqueline. "The Language of Nonsense in *Alice*." *Yale French Studies*, No. 43 (1969): 128-44.

Flescher details the many devices Carroll employs to create the nonsensical world of Wonderland.

Gardner, Martin. *The Annotated Alice*. W. W. Norton & Company, 2000.

Starting with the premise that Carroll's *Alice* books endure in modern times precisely because they appeal to adults more than children, Gardner's annotations presume a background in philosophy as well as mathematical and scientific theory.

Gray, Donald J., editor. *Alice in Wonderland*. A Norton Critical Edition, Second Edition, W. W. Norton & Company, 1992.

This edition contains useful annotations and several essays on *Alice* by such writers as Derek Hudson, Lewis Carroll, Gillian Avery, Peter Coveney, William Empson and Roger Henkle. The edition also contains many of Carroll's letters and diary entries.

Heath, Peter. The Philosopher's Alice: Alice's Adventures in Wonderland & Through the Looking Glass. St. Martin's Press, 1974.

Heath annotates Carroll's works with explanations of the philosophy he believes Carroll consciously espoused in both books.

Holmes, Roger W. "The Philosopher's 'Alice in Wonderland'." *Antioch Review*. Vol. XIX, No. 2 (Summer 1959).

Holmes examines Alice as a medieval Nominalist, who ascribes names to objects simply so as to not have to point. Elsewhere he writes that she displays pre-Socratic tendencies when she wonders where a candle's flame goes when it is blown out; and that the works' depiction of time indicates an affinity to the philosophy of Henri Bergson.

Kincaid, James R. "Alice's Invasion of Wonderland." *PMLA*, Vol. 88, No. 1 (January 1973): 92-99.

Kincaid believes that the Alice character gravitates between childish innocence and adolescent rebellion, revealing her as a symbol of childhood growing into adulthood.

Krutch, Joseph Wood. "Psychoanalyzing Alice." *The Nation*, Vol. 144, No. 5 (January 30, 1937): 129-30.

Krutch refutes the psychoanalytic remarks of Paul Schiller (annotated later in this section) by claiming the *Alice* books are more notable for their satirical depictions of Victorian England.

Matthews, Charles. "Satire in the *Alice* Books." *Criticism*, Vol. 12 (Winter 1970): 105-19.

Matthews believes much of *Alice* to be a satire of the restrictive atmosphere of Victorian England, particularly how those restrictions were arbitrarily and autocratically enforced against children.

Rackin, Donald. "Alice's Journey to the End of the Night." *PMLA* Vol. LXXXI (October 1966): 313-26.

In his essay, written to celebrate the centenary of the publication of *Alice's Adventures in Wonderland*, Rackin claims the importance and permanence of the book as a work of literature. Among the book's enduring features, asserts Rackin, is the theme of the nature of reality and humankind's perception of it.

Schilder, Paul. "Psychoanalytic Remarks on *Alice in Wonderland* and Lewis Carroll." *Journal of Nervous and Mental Diseases*, Vol. 87, No. 2 (February 1938): 159-68.

This famous article, originally delivered as a speech in 1936, postulates that the *Alice* books evidence a tremendous degree of anxiety and oral aggressiveness. Schilder concludes that Carroll's nonsense literature reveals its author's destructive tendencies.

Thomas, Donald. *Lewis Carroll: A Portrait with Background.* John Murray (Publishers) Ltd., 1996.

This recent biography reassesses Carroll's literary legacy, finding him to be a forerunner of modern linguistic studies and surrealism.

Van Doren, Mark, editor. "Lewis Carroll: *Alice in Wonderland*" in *The New Invitation to Learning.* Random House, 1942.

This article is a transcript of a radiobroadcast symposium conducted by Van Doren and featuring Katherine Anne Porter and Bertrand Russell. Russell argues that the book should be considered only for adults, while Porter concurs that it contains many frightening passages.

Wilson, Edmund. "C. L. Dodgson: The Poet Logician." *The Shores of Light: A Literary Chronicle of the Twenties and Thirties.* Farrar, Straus & Giroux, Inc. 1952.

This article, originally published in 1932, displays Wilson's belief that the *Alice* books are part of a large, consistent body of work that examines dream psychology and relativist theory.

Internet

"Illustrations of Lewis Carroll's *Alice's Adventures in Wonderland*"

www.exit109.com/~dnn/alice

This site is dedicated to illustrators other than John Tenniel, and features many full-color illustrations from such Georgian-era artists as Mabel Lucie Attwell, Bessie Pease Gutmann, Gwynedd M. Hudson, A. E. Jackson, Maria L. Kirk, and Arthur Rackham.

"Lewis Carroll Illustrated"

www.rust.net/~kdonohue/aliceidx.html

This site contains extensive information and links to other *Alice* and Carroll sites on many different *Alice*-related topics, including illustrations, costumes/performances, photographs, commercial images, and computer graphics. This site is a good place to visit first as it references many other sites that are more specific.

"Lewis Carroll Society of North America Home Page"

www.lewiscarroll.org

The "go-to" page for biographical information on Carroll, this site also features a bibliography of writings by and about Carroll and his works.

"Lewis Carroll: Teacher Resource File"

www.home.earthlink.net/~lfdean/carroll/index.html

Contains e-texts of much of Carroll's fiction and poetry and links to other sites containing biographical and critical essays.

"The Victorian Web"

www.landow.stg.brown.edu/victorian/victov.html

This site contains pages dedicated to Carroll's works, biography, visual arts, imagery, themes and social history with links to many essays on these topics as well as links to pages pertaining to other Victorian writers.

Films

Alice in Wonderland. Prod./dir. Cecil Hepworth. AIW. 1903.

This is the first film version of *Alice's Adventures in Wonderland.* Produced in England, this is a silent black and white film.

Alice in Wonderland. Dir. W. W. Young. American Film Company (1910), Nonpareil (1915). 1910, re-released 1915.

This silent film runs 28 minutes and features Viola Savoy as Alice.

Alice in Wonderland. Dir. Bud Pollard. Commonwealth Productions.1931.

This is the first cinematic version of *Alice* to feature sound; the running time is 55 minutes.

Alice in Wonderland. Dir. Norman McLeod. Paramount Pictures. 1933.

A light-hearted, major studio production, this cinematic version combines elements from both *Alice's Adventures in Wonderland* and *Through the Looking-Glass: And What Alice Found There* with a cast that includes W. C. Fields (Humpty Dumpty), Cary Grant (the Mock Turtle), and Gary Cooper (the White Knight). This version is also noted for its close adherence to the illustrations of John Tenniel.

Alice in Wonderland. Dir. Clyde Geronomi/Wilfred Jackson. Walt Disney Productions. 1951.

Featuring the voices of Ed Wynn (the Mad Hatter) and Sterling Holloway (the Cheshire Cat), this animated musical is noted for the quality of its illustrations and the songs "I'm Late" and "A Very Merry Un-Birthday."

Alice in Wonderland, or What's a Nice Kid Like You Doing in a Place Like This? Dir. Alex Levy. Hanna-Barbera Productions. 1966.

This musical version features hip, swinging performances by Sammy Davis, Jr., Liza Minnelli, and Zza Zza Gabor.

Alice in Wonderland. Dir. Jonathon Miller. BBC. 1967

This English version is noted for the high quality of the actors, including Sir John Gielgud, Sir Michael Redgrave, Peter Sellers, and Peter Cook, who perform the characters of Wonderland without costumes.

Alice's Adventures in Wonderland. Dir. William Sterling. British Television. 1972.

This musical version features Michael Crawford (the White Rabbit), Fiona Fullerton (Alice), Peter Sellers (the March Hare), Spike Milligan (the Gryphon), and Dudley Moore (the Dormouse) as Carroll's characters singing the songs of John Barry, best known as the composer of the James Bond theme.

Dreamchild. Dir. Gavin Millar. MGM. 1985.

A fictional depiction of Alice Liddell's trip to New York City in the 1930s, where the now elderly woman imagines she is reacquainted with the creatures from Wonderland.

Alice in Wonderland. Dir. Nick Willing. Hallmark Entertainment. 1999.

Featuring performances by Martin Short (the Mad Hatter), Ben Kingsley (the Caterpillar), and Whoopi Goldberg (the Cheshire Cat), this television adaptation also combines characters from both of Carroll's *Alice* books.

CLIFFSCOMPLETE READING GROUP DISCUSSION GUIDE

Use the following questions and topics to enhance your reading group discussions. The discussion can help get you thinking—and hopefully talking—about *Alice's Adventures in Wonderland* in a whole new way!

DISCUSSION QUESTIONS

1. *Alice's Adventures in Wonderland* is revealed at the end of the story to be a dream of the title character. Throughout the story few clues foreshadow the conclusion. Having read the story, is the reader prepared for the revelation that Alice is in a dream? Is the story believable as a dream?

2. *Alice's Adventures in Wonderland* contains two overt depictions of judicial proceedings. The first is in the Mouse's Tale, and the other in the trial of the Knave of Hearts. Is Carroll hinting at a deep contempt of the legal system of Victorian England? Do other instances in the work support or discredit this supposition?

3. From his childhood, Carroll was adept at mathematics. He was a lecturer in mathematics at Christ Church, Oxford, and was thought to be an uninspired writer on the subject. What bearing might this learning have on the subject matter of *Alice's Adventures in Wonderland?* Give examples from the novel.

4. G. K. Chesterton wrote that the quantity of critical commentary generated by Carroll's *Alice* books obscures the fact that Carroll wrote them to entertain children. Do you agree with Chesterton's assessment that the books are intended solely for children? Do you agree that the critical commentary on the works has gone too far in interpreting Carroll's intentions and personal life?

5. Carroll was an Anglican clergyman. Are there images, characters, or events in *Alice's Adventures in Wonderland* that indicate his Christian faith? List a few examples from the novel and describe how they indicate Carroll's Christian faith.

6. Much has been written about the dark psychological elements found in *Alice's Adventures in Wonderland*. Do you think that the book depicts fears common among children experiencing physical and mental growth? Use examples from the novel to support you argument.

7. William Empson wrote that Carroll was influenced by the concept of evolution as expounded in Charles Darwin's *The Origin of Species* before Carroll wrote *Alice's Adventures in Wonderland*. Are there any references to evolution beyond Chapter II? Give examples from the novel to support your answer.

8. *Alice's Adventures in Wonderland* is most often perceived as a Victorian novel. Is it possible to set the story in another time period and country while retaining the themes and manners so important to the story? For example, the tea party is germane to British culture. How would you rewrite this cultural phenomenon for a different time period and different social customs? How would you depict the lampoons of the English legal system and Victorian manners?

9. The use of puns, neologisms (a new word or a new meaning for an established word), and portmanteau words (a coined word that is a combination of two other words in form and meaning) by Carroll in *Alice's Adventures in Wonderland* indicates a tremendous grasp of the English language. Explain why translating Alice—especially Carroll's wordplay—into another language would be difficult.

10. Film and television adaptations of *Alice's Adventures in Wonderland* invariably include scenes and characters from the book's sequel, *Through the Looking-Glass: And What Alice Found There*. Indeed, *Alice's Adventures in Wonderland* consists of only 25,000 words. Explain the reasons why filmmakers rarely mount a full-length cinematic production using only the original *Alice*.

Notes

Index

Notes

Notes

Notes

CliffsNotes™

CLIFFSCOMPLETE

Hamlet
Julius Caesar
King Henry IV, Part I
King Lear
Macbeth
The Merchant of Venice
Othello
Romeo and Juliet
The Tempest
Twelfth Night

Look for Other Series in the CliffsNotes Family

LITERATURE NOTES

Absalom, Absalom!
The Aeneid
Agamemnon
Alice in Wonderland
All the King's Men
All the Pretty Horses
All Quiet on the Western Front
All's Well & Merry Wives
American Poets of the
   20th Century
American Tragedy
Animal Farm
Anna Karenina
Anthem
Antony and Cleopatra
Aristotle's Ethics
As I Lay Dying
The Assistant
As You Like It
Atlas Shrugged
Autobiography of Ben Franklin
Autobiography of Malcolm X
The Awakening
Babbit
Bartleby & Benito Cereno
The Bean Trees
The Bear
The Bell Jar
Beloved
Beowulf
The Bible
Billy Budd & Typee
Black Boy
Black Like Me

Bleak House
Bless Me, Ultima
The Bluest Eye & Sula
Brave New World
The Brothers Karamazov
The Call of the Wild &
   White Fang
Candide
The Canterbury Tales
Catch-22
Catcher in the Rye
The Chosen
The Color Purple
Comedy of Errors…
Connecticut Yankee
The Contender
The Count of Monte Cristo
Crime and Punishment
The Crucible
Cry, the Beloved Country
Cyrano de Bergerac
Daisy Miller & Turn…Screw
David Copperfield
Death of a Salesman
The Deerslayer
Diary of Anne Frank
Divine Comedy-I. Inferno
Divine Comedy-II. Purgatorio
Divine Comedy-III. Paradiso
Doctor Faustus
Dr. Jekyll and Mr. Hyde
Don Juan
Don Quixote
Dracula
Electra & Medea
Emerson's Essays
Emily Dickinson Poems
Emma
Ethan Frome
The Faerie Queene
Fahrenheit 451
Far from the Madding Crowd
A Farewell to Arms
Farewell to Manzanar
Fathers and Sons
Faulkner's Short Stories
Faust Pt. I & Pt. II
The Federalist
Flowers for Algernon
For Whom the Bell Tolls
The Fountainhead
Frankenstein
The French Lieutenant's Woman
The Giver
Glass Menagerie & Streetcar
Go Down, Moses
The Good Earth

The Grapes of Wrath
Great Expectations
The Great Gatsby
Greek Classics
Gulliver's Travels
Hamlet
The Handmaid's Tale
Hard Times
Heart of Darkness & Secret Sharer
Hemingway's Short Stories
Henry IV Part 1
Henry IV Part 2
Henry V
House Made of Dawn
The House of the
   Seven Gables
Huckleberry Finn
I Know Why the Caged Bird Sings
Ibsen's Plays I
Ibsen's Plays II
The Idiot
Idylls of the King
The Iliad
Incidents in the Life of a Slave Girl
Inherit the Wind
Invisible Man
Ivanhoe
Jane Eyre
Joseph Andrews
The Joy Luck Club
Jude the Obscure
Julius Caesar
The Jungle
Kafka's Short Stories
Keats & Shelley
The Killer Angels
King Lear
The Kitchen God's Wife
The Last of the Mohicans
Le Morte d'Arthur
Leaves of Grass
Les Miserables
A Lesson Before Dying
Light in August
The Light in the Forest
Lord Jim
Lord of the Flies
The Lord of the Rings
Lost Horizon
Lysistrata & Other Comedies
Macbeth
Madame Bovary
Main Street
The Mayor of Casterbridge
Measure for Measure
The Merchant of Venice
Middlemarch

A Midsummer Night's Dream
The Mill on the Floss
Moby-Dick
Moll Flanders
Mrs. Dalloway
Much Ado About Nothing
My Ántonia
Mythology
Narr. …Frederick Douglass
Native Son
New Testament
Night
1984
Notes from the Underground
The Odyssey
Oedipus Trilogy
Of Human Bondage
Of Mice and Men
The Old Man and the Sea
Old Testament
Oliver Twist
The Once and Future King
One Day in the Life of
   Ivan Denisovich
One Flew Over
   the Cuckoo's Nest
100 Years of Solitude
O'Neill's Plays
Othello
Our Town
The Outsiders
The Ox Bow Incident
Paradise Lost
A Passage to India
The Pearl
The Pickwick Papers
The Picture of Dorian Gray
Pilgrim's Progress
The Plague
Plato's Euthyphro…
Plato's The Republic
Poe's Short Stories
A Portrait of the Artist…
The Portrait of a Lady
The Power and the Glory
Pride and Prejudice
The Prince
The Prince and the Pauper
A Raisin in the Sun
The Red Badge of Courage
The Red Pony
The Return of the Native
Richard II
Richard III
The Rise of Silas Lapham
Robinson Crusoe